On Dolphin Bay

Richard Clark

Praise for Richard Clark's Books

'Clark is particularly good on the colours, flavours and scents of Greece. He has got under the skin of the place in a way few outsiders have been able to.'

Mark Hudson, winner of Somerset Maugham Award, Thomas Cook Travel Book Award and the Samuel Johnson Prize

'Richard Clark captures the spirit of Greece I love. His books make me long to see the places he describes.'

Jennifer Barclay, author of *Falling in Honey, An Octopus in My Ouzo, Wild Abandon* and *Taverna by the Sea*

'There is poetry in Richard Clark's words and through his eyes. I recommend anyone missing Greece, visiting Greece or just wishing they could go to Greece to take a look!'

Sara Alexi, author of *The Greek Village Series*

'Thanks, Richard, for adding your great eye to your gifted pen in service to sharing the essence of Greece with the world!'

Jeffrey Siger, bestselling, award-winning US crime writer

'Richard Clark writes with great authority and a deep affection for his subject, which comes from his long association with Greece… Excellent.'

Marjory McGinn, author of *The Peloponnese Series, A Saint for the Summer* and *How Greek is Your Love?*

'Return to Turtle Beach is a heart-warming story that will transport you to the enchanting island of Crete.'

Maria A. Karamitsos, *My Greek Books*

'In *The Forgotten Song* the author weaves his magical prose to take the reader on a romantic journey with more twists and turns than a Cretan mountain pass.'

Tony Prouse, author and journalist

'There are moments when this book [*The Crete Walking Society*] literally took my breath away! Sometimes with the beautifully captured images of Crete and sometimes the powerful feelings brought to life in the characters. Richard Clark is firmly one of my all-time favourite authors. His books are so beautifully written and an absolute joy to read.'

Angie Fox Lane

'Richard has a writing style that transports you to the real Greece. I truly love his ability to take me with him to wonderful places, feel the warmth of the Greek sunshine and experience Greece through the eyes of his characters. For me, he is one of the best writers out there.'

Peter Barber, author of *A Parthenon on Our Roof*, *A Parthenon in Pefki* and *The Parthenon Paradox*

[*A Piano Bar in Crete* is] 'a poignant modern story, brilliantly crafted, with universal appeal.'

Suzi Stembridge, author

[*The Vineyard in Crete* is] 'a compelling and poignant story of forbidden love, revenge and reconciliation, once more infused with the author's rich talent for bringing all things Cretan vividly to life through his wonderfully evocative prose.'

Tony Prouse, author and journalist

By the Same Author

The Vineyard in Crete

A Piano Bar in Crete

The Crete Walking Society

The Forgotten Song

Return to Turtle Beach

The Lost Lyra

The Greek Islands – A Notebook

Crete – A Notebook

Rhodes – A Notebook

Corfu – A Notebook

Hidden Crete – A Notebook

More Hidden Crete – A Notebook

Eastern Crete – A Notebook

Richard Clark's Greek Islands Anthology

The Crete Trilogy

On Dolphin Bay

First published in America and Great Britain 2025

Copyright © Richard Clark 2025

Cover design © Mike Parsons 2025

All rights reserved. No part of this publication can be reproduced or transmitted in any form or by any means, electronic or mechanical, without permission in writing from Richard Clark.

Richard Clark has asserted his right to be identified as the author of this work in accordance with the Copyright, Designs and Patents Act, 1988

ISBN – 9798284993712

www.facebook.com/richardclarkbooks

https://notesfromgreece.com

About the Author

Richard Clark is a writer, editor and journalist who has worked on an array of national newspapers and magazines in the UK. In 1982, on a whim, he decided to up sticks and live on the Greek island of Crete. So began a love affair that has continued to this day, and he still visits the Greek islands, where he has a home, on a regular basis. In 2016, he gave up the daily commute to London to become a full-time author. He is married with two grown-up children and five grandchildren, and lives in Kent.

Acknowledgements

This book is a work of fiction, and although some real places have lent themselves as locations, many are the product of my imagination. All the characters are fictitious, and any resemblance to real persons, living or dead, is purely coincidental. Any mistakes are mine.

A huge thank you goes to my friends Tony and Bernadette Prouse for their guidance. I am also grateful to the author Yvonne Payne for reading and giving her comments on the manuscript.

As always, I am lucky to be edited by the incredible Jennifer Barclay who has made this book so much better than it otherwise might have been. Again I am grateful to Mike Parsons for his beautiful cover design and illustrations. Lastly, I must thank my family, Denise, Rebecca, James, Pete, Lucy, Esther, Imogen, Iris, Douglas and Edward for their unending support.

Note

The names of male Greek characters ending in an 's' will drop the letter in the vocative case (when that character is being addressed in direct speech).

To Fanis and Maria, whose support keeps the dream alive, and Katerina and Giannis for many glorious days spent out on the bay.

Prologue

2004

THE BOY PUSHED the mask over his forehead and rolled onto his back. In the salty water he floated weightlessly, closing his eyes against the relentless afternoon sun. His ears under the surface, he loved the silence. The warm sea relaxed every muscle in his body. For minutes he lay suspended in the bay, away from the excited laughter of other children playing on the beach across the causeway, where his parents had hired two sun beds and were reading in the shade of an umbrella.

It was his first time abroad, the journey an adventure in itself. To begin with he had been a bit nervous of flying but he had loved the sensation of the plane taking off and rising above the clouds into the blue. Amazed, he thought he could make out the slight curvature of the earth. As they crossed the Alps, he stared down in wonder at the snowy mountains. Getting closer to Crete, as the aircraft began to descend he was transfixed by the bluest of blue seas dotted with islands. He loved the rollercoaster sensation of the plane touching down, being pushed back in his seat as the brakes were applied.

When the cabin doors opened, it was as though he had been released into a whole new world. Everything looked brighter and the air smelled of exotic herbs. At the bottom of the steps which descended from the aircraft he turned and saw the sea stretching away to the horizon. He had never experienced anything so... well, so blue was all he could think of to describe it to himself.

That had been the previous day. But already it felt like aeons ago. After the long journey, his parents were tired. Following a gyros dinner at a taverna in the square they had returned to their apartment. The little of what he had seen of Elounda that previous night had filled his dreams with glorious anticipation. As he awakened to the early morning sunshine and jumped out of bed and onto the balcony, what was revealed was more than he could have imagined. Not a stone's throw from where he stood was the bay. The still water was bordered by a hilly island, and a bridge joined the island to a road which looked as though it was floating on the sea. Beside this was a beach dotted with tamarisk trees.

When his parents proposed a lazy day at the beach, Jack was more than happy. He was a strong swimmer and was excited when his dad took him to the shops and bought them both masks and tubes and promised to teach him to snorkel. It had taken him no time to master how to angle the tube and clear it on resurfacing after a dive, and being able to swim under the water with eyes wide open revealed a whole new world. Shoals of silver fish swam amongst the rocks and an octopus scuttled across a patch of sandy seabed to find refuge in its garden.

He loved swimming. Since he had been a baby, his father had taken him most Saturday mornings to the local pool, and in no time he was confident in the water. At eight years old, to him it was a natural environment.

'Those are the Venetian salt flats which were used up until as recently as the 1970s,' his father had announced, reading from his guidebook and pointing.

Jack could see what he thought was a heron standing on one leg on a partly submerged wall which separated two shallow lakes which must have been the saltpans.

'And further up there on the other side of the road it says is the sunken city of Olous,' his father continued. 'An ancient settlement since Minoan times, it is thought to have sunk beneath the waves due to earthquakes.'

Jack's eyes followed the causeway to the bridge, beside which were the remains of what looked like windmills without their sails.

'Can I go and find the sunken city?' Jack asked. His mother lowered her sunglasses and looked at the flat calm sea on the other side of the road. 'I don't see why not, as long as you don't swim too far out.'

'From what it says in my book, the submerged city is close inshore,' his father pointed.

Jack crossed the road and put his towel on a rock. Entering the water, he could see little apart from patches of sand and weed on the seabed. As he swam further out he began to make out lines of rocks just a few feet below, where the foundations of the city walls must have been. He dived down and touched them, before resurfacing, clearing his snorkel tube and floating on the surface, picturing what the ancient city must have been like. Where now a shoal of silver fish foraged for food amongst the weed that clung to the millennia-old remains, he imagined people going about their daily business. Jack floated, entranced. In the silence his mind focused on the shapes and details of a long gone past, connected to the present by what lay beneath him. His eyes stopped on something tiny, wedged between two stones. Taking a deep breath he dived down, kicking his legs hard. The fish scattered as he reached out. Grabbing it between his fingers he resurfaced, blowing water from his tube before taking a deep breath. Removing his mask, he looked at the piece of metal he'd retrieved. He needed to get back to where he could touch the seabed with his feet to examine it. He put his find in the pocket of his shorts and swam towards the shore until it was shallow enough to stand up.

Rubbing the metal and picking at it with his fingers he could see it was an old coin. Closer inspection revealed the face of a woman. His head buzzing he flipped it over and could make out the shape of a leaping dolphin. The thought that he had discovered hidden treasure filled Jack with excitement. He could hardly wait to return to the beach and show his parents what he had found.

'Catch it!' Jack heard a shout. Something hit him on the back of the head. It was soft but the shock was enough to make him drop the coin as a large beach inflatable blew past him.

Chapter 1

2019

THE DAMP GRASS soaked through his shirt. Jack lay staring upwards. The summer night had turned cool, a respite from the sweaty pubs and clubs he had found himself in earlier. He relished the silence as he stared up at the stars and took comfort from how small he felt. He closed his eyes and fell asleep.

'Are you alright?' A hand touched his shoulder. He opened one eye and then the other. Bending over him, a young woman pushed back her long dark hair revealing deep brown eyes which showed the concern he could detect in her soft voice.

'I'm fine,' he pushed himself up into a sitting position. 'Just having a rest.'

'You don't feel sick? If you do, you should lie on your side.'

As he began to come round, Jack took in the woman looking down at him. He thought her white dress rather formal and her high-heeled shoes had sunk into the grass but he could not fail to notice she was beautiful.

'What are you?' he asked getting to his feet and smiling. 'A doctor?'

As soon as the words left his mouth, Jack worried that he had been rude.

'Well, actually, I suppose as of today, I kind of am. I'm Georgia by the way,' her smile reassuring Jack that she had not taken offence.

'I'm sorry. I'm Jack.' He held out his hand. 'I'm afraid as you can probably tell I've been out celebrating the end of my student life. Tomorrow the real world begins.'

'Rather scary, isn't it,' said Georgia. 'Seriously though, are you OK? You looked out for the count.'

'I'm fine, really. But it was kind of you to check. Have you been out partying too?'

'Yes, last day. Tomorrow, or rather today I go back to my parents', and in a few weeks I start my foundation training at the local hospital. And you?'

'Nothing so worthy I'm afraid. I'm off on holiday before I start an internship my father wangled for me at the newspaper he works on. How he managed that I don't know. I can barely write my name, just scraped a third in English.'

'So you want to be a journalist?' Georgia appeared genuinely interested in something which Jack had barely considered himself. Yet that was all too soon to become the reality of the course in life he was embarking on.

'I don't know really. It's what my dad does and I guess if I can do anything it is write. That's what some of my lecturers have told me anyway. It's just that whenever I take exams the stress kills me and I freeze. How I even got a degree amazes me. If it hadn't been for coursework I would have been in trouble.'

Now he was standing, he noticed she barely reached his shoulders. 'So you're, sorry, were, a medical student. A doctor now?'

'Still years more training, but yes I am. If I'm honest it frightens me a little. It's all a bit grown up.' Georgia looked down at the ground.

'I know what you mean. But at least you've got a vocation. Part of me doesn't want to leave Exeter, but there's no way I could get on a post grad course with my results. It's out into the real world for me.' There was something about the young medic which made Jack want to keep talking to her. 'Isn't it strange that we've been here for three years and our paths never crossed?'

'It's been five years for me,' replied Georgia. 'You must be younger than I am?'

'No, I took two years out. I tell people they were gap years, but really they were going to a crammer college in Brighton to do re-takes of my A Levels so I could get in here. Eventually they relented and gave me a place.'

Georgia smiled. She did not know what it was about the tall, slightly awkward, diffident man she found herself in conversation with, but there was something that she warmed to.

'What time are you leaving?' Jack asked.

'Mum and Dad are picking me up about lunchtime.' Georgia glanced at her watch. It was already approaching four thirty in the morning.

'I'm catching the train, so it really doesn't matter when I leave, we don't go on holiday until tomorrow.' Jack hesitated. 'Do you fancy getting some breakfast? I know a café that opens early in Topsham for the fishermen and sailors.'

'Why not, it's too late to go to bed and I could do with some carbs.'

Both of them were reluctant to let the moment go.

'I don't think either of us is fit for a six-mile hike,' she continued, 'but there must be taxis about sweeping up the debris from last night.'

Georgia was right, and they almost immediately found a cab dropping off at St Luke's college.

The sun was rising as they drew up in the small estuary town of Topsham. Already on the jetties and the midstream moorings early-rising yachtsmen were busying themselves to make the morning tide. Deep in conversation, the pair walked through the narrow streets of old seafarers' cottages and along the waterfront. To Jack the moment was perfect. He reached in his pocket for his phone and took a picture of them both, him slightly dishevelled but happy, her smiling in her posh frock and heels.

Over a cooked breakfast they made easy conversation about their past, their time at university and hopes for the future. It appeared to Jack that his new friend's career was all mapped out. She would have to do two years of foundation training as a junior doctor before choosing a specialism to study to further her career. For Jack things were less certain. He had little idea of what this internship on a prestigious broadsheet newspaper might entail. He would worry about that after he returned from

Crete, a fortnight with his parents in the holiday home they had recently bought in a village near Elounda.

'It's a small world!' Georgia was amazed when Jack told her where he was going on holiday. 'My father's from Crete, from the southwest in Paleochora. My grandmother still lives there. Dad's a doctor too and moved here in the early nineties, met my mother and here I am. We used to go there on holiday a lot when I was younger, but what with my studies I haven't been for a few years. I've been to Elounda though, that's near Spinalonga isn't it?'

'Yes it is. What a coincidence.' Jack looked across the Formica-topped table at the beautiful woman who sat opposite and she returned his gaze. 'Where my parents have bought a house is in Epano Elounda on the mountainside looking down on the Bay of Korfos, near Spinalonga. We went there when I was a kid and my parents loved it so much we kept going back. It's my happy place too, I can't wait to return. I suppose Dad is starting to think about retirement now and wants to spend more time there. I haven't seen the house yet but Mum and Dad tell me it's been beautifully renovated. This will be my first visit. Do you speak Greek?'

'I do, but it's a bit rusty. Dad was always keen that I learn, and speaks Greek to me when we are together. I think he would like to move back to Crete some day.'

Jack found himself talking to Georgia with an openness he had rarely felt. Her sparkling eyes and smile put him at ease. He was already aware of time running out as their chance meeting would soon have to come to an end.

They caught a bus back to Exeter and made their farewells on the lawn outside St Luke's college where hours before they had met. As they said goodbye and good luck and exchanged phone numbers, both wanted to kiss but neither dared cross that boundary. They settled for a hug. As he walked away, Jack turned and looked at the olive-skinned girl who raised a hand and swept her long black hair from her face, smiled and waved. He could not help feeling sad that he had lost something he could never replace.

Alone, he began to walk back to the house he had shared with two fellow students. Tiredness caught up with him. The buoyant mood he had felt in the company of Georgia drained away. He tried to lift his mood by thinking about his holiday to Crete but couldn't feel anything except anxiety about his future. He knocked on the bedroom doors of his housemates but there was silence. Jack packed his few belongings in a small case and a holdall. He dialled Georgia's number, but his call went straight to voicemail. He hung up, picked up his bags and left, closing the door on his student life.

He slept through most of the journey from Exeter to Waterloo. In his dreams and in his waking moments he could not rid his mind of the alluring woman he had all too briefly met. As he got off the train and crossed the station to Waterloo East, he took a moment to look forward to going to Greece.

As the train rumbled through the Kent countryside, Jack felt reassured by the familiarity of the area he had grown up in. He loved returning home. There he felt safe and secure. His parents had moved to the countryside before he was born, and since he could remember his father, Stephen, had taken the daily commute to London for his work as a newspaper journalist. His mother, Ginny, had worked as a teacher in the local primary school he had attended as a child until she recently took early retirement.

His parents had always given him free rein, the time and space he needed to plot a path through the world. They fiercely supported his independence but were always there with a helping hand when it was needed. He knew he appeared laid-back with an easy intelligence but had always struggled in situations he couldn't control. His school years had been difficult. He found it hard to concentrate when under pressure, something which had exasperated his teachers as he was consistently unable to achieve the exam grades they predicted for him and in formal interviews his heart would race and his mind go blank.

But somehow his parents had managed to steer him through it all, nudging him towards studying subjects he was naturally good at and at which he could be judged by continual assessment. Late in his school career he had been diagnosed with ADHD, but with his parents' help he had managed to secure a place at university and now had a degree and an internship on a national newspaper. He would worry about that when he returned from holiday. In the meantime he was off to Crete the following day.

They'd been going to Elounda on holiday for years, and finally, a few months ago, his parents had completed the purchase of a traditional house in the sleepy village of Epano Elounda, about a mile up into the mountains. Dad had sent him pictures, but he couldn't wait to see it for himself.

At the station his dad welcomed him with a hug. 'Congratulations on graduating. Your mum and I thought it best to celebrate when we get to Crete, we've got an early start.'

'I think that's a good idea. I didn't get much sleep last night,' Jack agreed. 'I can't believe my university years are over, and that I got through it. I couldn't have done it without you and mum's support. Thank you for everything.'

Stephen drove them through the narrow country lanes to the village house which Jack had called home his whole life. As they parked on the gravel drive, Ginny stepped out of the front door to welcome her son. She was tall like Jack, her blond hair, slightly greying, was cut in a neat bob, her face was beaming at the thought of having him home. 'I'm so proud of you, Jack. Well done! Does it feel good to be back?' she gushed.

Over an early dinner his parents talked excitedly about the house they had bought. Jack shared their enthusiasm but tiredness was catching up with him. Having to leave for the airport well before dawn to catch the seven o'clock flight, he would suffer the following day if he did not get some sleep. He said goodnight and went to his room, emptied the holdall of dirty washing and stuffed it with clean clothes, set an alarm for two-thirty and went to bed. In his mind he pictured Georgia's smiling face as he drifted off to sleep.

*

Jack dozed on the flight to Heraklion, his sleep punctuated by the interruptions of the cabin crew asking if he would like food, drink or duty-free items from the trolley. He offered to drive the hire car from the airport, but his father could see he was exhausted and took the wheel. Jack loved the journey east to Elounda, which since his childhood had been filled with so much promise for the holiday ahead, but in the heat he was fighting with his eyes and when he awoke his father was just turning off the main highway.

He opened the car window and let the warm air rush over him. He could smell the herbs and flowers growing on the hillsides and see the Bay of Mirabello glistening in the afternoon sun. He knew what was coming as they completed the long climb up the hillside from Agios Nikolaos and topped the mountain. However many times he had seen it, the view of Elounda never ceased to bring a smile to his face.

Beneath them lay the Bay of Korfos, shimmering in the afternoon heat, a few yachts at anchor and ferries criss-crossing to and from Spinalonga. He could see the causeway to the island of Kalidon and the bridge which connected it to Elounda. He could make out the beaches on which he had spent so many happy days. A caique was at rest above the sunken city of Olous.

The road flattened out and narrowed as they approached Elounda. His father found a parking space in the square on the waterfront and went to the supermarket to buy water, wine and snacks. Then they headed out of the town and up a mountain road which twisted its way through olive groves and smallholdings as it climbed steeply, the view getting more and more spectacular.

They passed a road sign announcing Epano Elounda and kept driving higher up into the village before his father brought the car to rest in a parking space beside a church.

'We're here,' said Stephen, opening the car door and stretching his legs. 'The village streets are a bit narrow for me to drive in, and the footpath there takes us right to the front door. We'll take what we can of the luggage and come back for the rest.'

'I can manage the shopping,' insisted Ginny. 'If you take the cases we'll do it in one. It's a bit hot to be walking to and fro.'

The path led between old stone houses shaded by lemon, fig and carob trees. On a corner, they stopped outside a white house, its blue shutters closed. Stephen searched in his pocket for the key and opened the door. Stepping inside, the house was cool, and Jack felt the relief from the mid-afternoon heat outside. At first it was dark and difficult to see but light poured in when the curtains, windows and shutters were opened to reveal the beautifully restored interior. Standing for a moment he took in the large sitting area with a fireplace, the tiled floor rising up three steps to a kitchen with a bathroom beyond.

He followed as his parents proudly led him up the staircase to the first floor, past a bedroom and through an upstairs sitting room, opening the curtains and then a door which led out onto a large terrace. Outside, Jack could see the true wonder of the house. The sun-drenched terrace was half covered with a large pergola up which grew a red bougainvillea exploding with blooms. Stepping out from the shade, the open part of the terrace was bathed in sunlight and was surrounded by a wall. Below, the roofs of the village houses met the groves of olive trees which blanketed the mountainside as it swept down towards the bay. Beneath him he could see Elounda glinting in the sunshine, and the endless sea, and in the distant heat haze the outline of the mountains which hugged the coast all the way to the eastern end of the island.

'Wow!' Jack could not take his eyes off the view. 'I can see why you chose here. I mean, the house is beautiful in itself. But this view… you could never grow tired of that.'

'I'm pleased you like it,' said Ginny. We fell in love with the house the moment we saw it, and when we came up here, it sealed the deal. Anyway, it's here whenever you want to use it.'

Stephen handed a key to his son. 'We had this cut for you.'

A broad grin spread across Jack's face. 'Thanks, Dad. Thanks, Mum.' Jack hugged both his parents in turn and was filled with a warm sense of security.

'First things first, let's open a bottle of that wine and drink a toast to congratulate you on your graduation and all the happy times we'll have here in Crete.'

Chapter 2

2019

GEORGIA STOPPED TO take in the moment. She could feel the July rain trickling down her neck. She ignored the damp patch spreading across the back of her new white blouse and allowed herself to take in the emotions of starting her first day working in the career she had for so long dreamed about. In front of her was the main entrance to the hospital where her mother, Christine, also worked as a theatre sister. She contemplated the doors she had passed through before on numerous occasions, and felt butterflies in her stomach. This time it was the start of her new life. She would spend at least two years there doing her rotations before deciding on which branch of medicine she wanted to specialise in.

She had chosen the Royal Cornwall Hospital in Truro as it was just over a half-hour's drive from the village she had grown up in, where her parents still lived. Moving back home, she hoped she could save some money and make inroads into paying off her student loan. She loved walking in the surrounding countryside and hoped that would be the perfect antidote to the stresses of her work, which her parents would understand; as well as her mother working in the hospital her father, Nikos, was a GP in a larger village nearby.

Inside the doors, she unzipped her jacket, smoothed down the front of her dark grey trousers, took a deep breath and headed down the corridor towards the start of her new life as a doctor.

*

From that first day the work was hard, but Georgia relished the challenges and took satisfaction in the knowledge that she was making a difference to people's lives, and over her first few months of training she settled into a routine.

She was pleased with the knowledge she had absorbed at university but aware of how much she still had to learn. When she returned home after her shifts at the hospital, she would eat the meal her mother had prepared, sometimes a dinner, sometimes breakfast, and retire to her room to study until she gave in to sleep. Her parents were both aware of the rigours of the work from their own experience. On those glorious days when Georgia was not working they would go out for picnics or drive to the seaside at St Ives or Mevagissey.

Occasionally she would get a text message from Jack and would smile at the memory of the handsome man she had met so fleetingly in the last hours of her time at university. Already those days seemed a long time ago, and with time the messages petered out.

Christine and Nikos loved having her back home after the years away. For Georgia, it was good to have the reassurance of her parents when she had had a bad day, although even in the toughest moments she never regretted her choice of profession.

Several months after she had started her training, Georgia found love. It began with smiles on the corridors and hospital wards. Georgia immediately warmed to the tall, blond surgical registrar; the sight of his dazzling blue eyes greeting her would brighten any day. The looks became words and instead of passing each other they began to stop and talk. As time went by, Georgia found herself encountering the young surgeon more often when she visited the canteen. He introduced himself as Rory, and if they bumped into each other would sit and drink coffee together. Georgia was delighted when he plucked up the courage to ask her out on a date, drinks and lunch in a country pub. Despite the difficulties of finding time together their relationship blossomed and Georgia couldn't have been happier.

*

It was six months into her training that the first news stories began to appear. Around the coffee machines and water coolers in the hospital, whispers of a new disease that had started in China began to be discussed. As the weeks went by, the Coronavirus that had been little more than a distant news story got closer. Soon, with every day that passed the news got more frenzied until the first cases were reported in the UK, and then the first deaths. Seriously sick patients were arriving at hospitals across the country, including Truro.

As the pandemic took hold, trainee doctors were asked to volunteer to care for the sick despite woeful shortages of protective equipment. Georgia did not hesitate to step up and make herself available. She was young and saw it as her duty to help, although in the few moments she was not rushed off her feet she had to admit she was frightened. Her father was working from home doing consultations over the phone and when he was not doing that, he volunteered his help at the hospital.

In those dark days, moments with Rory were snatched. In the midst of those uncertain times, in the hospital the fight against the disease was like a war and the intensity of their relationship was heightened by the jeopardy they faced every day.

Every Thursday night people would come out of their front doors and clap in appreciation of the selfless work done by front line workers and every day the death toll rose. The disease seemed relentless and the waves of admissions to hospital threatened to overwhelm the staff. Like many, Georgia succumbed to the virus. For her, the symptoms were unpleasant but not severe.

Days later Rory showed symptoms and a test confirmed he had the disease. His decline was rapid. Within two days he was admitted as a patient to the very ward where previously he had been treating the sick. None of the drugs administered worked and the decision was made to put him into an induced coma on a ventilator. A week later Rory was dead.

At first Georgia was numb. She had not met her boyfriend's parents and was unsure they even knew of her existence. With the laws limiting those attending, she did not go to the funeral. She was keen to return to work as soon as possible to fight the disease which had killed her lover and to take her mind off her loss.

Yet as weeks went by, she could not throw off the malaise and regain the energy she had previously emanated. She could feel herself sliding into a pit of despair and there was nothing she could grasp that would stop her from falling.

Whilst the powers that be flip-flopped over policy, the only light at the end of the tunnel was the vaccines which had been developed at unprecedented speed. The first jabs were put in people's arms in the days before the first Christmas, but it was not until months afterwards that things began to return to some sort of normality. In hospitals up and down the country, however, the staff were exhausted, many traumatised, and the backlog of patients was never-ending. People had long since given up clapping on their doorsteps. Despite the pandemic being over, the sick were dying waiting for ambulances. In hospitals patients languished on trolleys in corridors and waiting lists of people awaiting surgery grew longer. It was clear to anyone who worked in healthcare that the system and many of the staff who worked in it were broken. Meanwhile, politicians had now turned their attention to defending their breaking of the laws they had imposed during the pandemic. Whilst those in government bickered, they didn't consider the radical solutions required to rescue the health service.

By the time Covid restrictions in the outside world were lifted, Georgia had finished her foundation course. She had elected and was accepted to train in Emergency medicine, and embarked on the long haul of training while working in the Casualty department. If life outside the hospital walls was getting back to the way it had been, and many of the risks to the medical staff had been relieved, the working days were just as intense.

The tail of Covid was never-ending and there were more and more sick patients arriving in Emergency departments. The wait for treatment and the insecurity felt by the public had turned their gratitude towards health workers to frustration at a broken service unable to cope with demand. Morale was at an all-time low and doctors and nurses felt undervalued by a government which until recently had been singing their praises. For Georgia, along with many of her colleagues, the knowledge that they were unable to give the best and fastest treatment to their patients gnawed away at them.

Depression crept up on Georgia slowly. The anger she had felt at the death of Rory she had fended off by battling the disease which had killed him. But as time went by the grief at his passing began to grip her like a clenched fist. On her days off she found it increasingly difficult to motivate herself to see friends or go out in the countryside. Her parents could see the decline, but struggled to find a way to lift her mood.

Every night she went to bed exhausted, but sleep would not come. She could not empty her head of thoughts of Rory, her work and the patients who were being let down. When fatigue finally claimed her, she would awake dazed from sleep, irritated by the alarm she had now taken to setting. She forced herself to rise, heavy-headed and dreading the day ahead. When she did not need to go into the hospital she would try to walk in the woods around the village. She knew that the fresh air and exercise were good for her wellbeing but all too often she found it difficult to let the beauty of the landscape soothe her senses as her mind would focus on her feeling of hopelessness.

When she didn't feel like getting out, it was often their family dog, Roger, who persuaded her. Despite his advancing years, the English Pointer had boundless energy and she could not resist his eyes entreating her to take him for a walk. He would run for miles in the woods, always returning to her whistle, and the hours she spent out with him became one of the few times she found solace.

Her parents worried, but when they broached the subject of how she was feeling she tried to cover up her anxiety, putting on a brave face and insisting she was OK. They weren't fooled, but it was difficult to know what to do for the best. They just had to hope that things might improve.

*

The May sun seeped through the curtains. Georgia could hear her mum and dad downstairs making coffee. She turned over and pulled the duvet over her head to shut out the world. She had hardly slept and was desperate for rest. She closed her eyes and willed herself to sleep. She had a day off and could stay in bed as long as she wanted.

'Get off, Roger,' she mumbled, feeling a cold, wet nose and a lick on her face as the dog buried his head beneath the duvet. Georgia held the quilt tight to repel the friendly invasion, but knew it would be in vain. Reluctantly she swung her legs out of bed. Roger now sat on the floor staring at her, his tail sweeping the carpet.

'Alright, I get the hint. Let me get a shower first.'

Roger was waiting outside the bathroom door when she emerged. Her head was still hazy and she felt exhausted. Perhaps a walk would blow away the cobwebs. She declined her mother's offer of a coffee before slipping the lead around Roger's neck and opening the door. The sun was already warm; a robin left its perch on a fence post and flew across the blue sky. Georgia barely took notice, her head bowed to the familiar path that headed into the woods. Roger nudged her leg and she bent down, loosened the leash and pulled it over the dog's ears. Immediately he bounded off into the trees and for a moment Georgia raised her head and watched his progress before she returned her gaze to the ground and laboured up the trail.

It was on this path that they found her, hugging her knees to her chin, in a tight ball and rocking backwards and forwards, sobbing. Roger had run home and barked at the door then led Georgia's parents to the woods, where they discovered her, inconsolable.

She could just about recall her parents trying to get her home, one on either side of her and the dog inches behind. She was put to bed and an appointment made to see her GP. It was obvious that she could not return to her job at the hospital any time soon and she was signed off. Her parents tried to access counselling, but as with so many of their services the NHS was overstretched and unable to provide help, even to their own staff. Her father found a private clinical psychologist who could take on the case.

In her therapy sessions Georgia began to understand that the thoughts of hopelessness that she often felt at work, that had led to her collapsing into depression and withdrawing from her family and friends, were not caused by her own inadequacies but by things outside her control. With the help of the therapist she learned to be kinder to herself and to reevaluate the things that were important to her. Slowly, day by day, week by week, month by month, they began to put the pieces back together. She learned that she had not lost the desire to help people, but one thing became clear: the frustration of battling to make a difference in her current job was having a disastrous effect on her wellbeing.

Since her breakdown, Roger had taken to sleeping on her bed. In the days when she found it difficult to speak to anyone and did not want to get up, she took comfort from his lying next to her. As she started to engage more with the world, if she was reluctant to rise in the morning Roger would go downstairs and return with his lead in his mouth, rousing her to take him out for a run.

On those walks Georgia tried to put into practice the techniques she was learning with her therapist. Slowly she learned how to appreciate what was around her as she meandered for hours along the paths which crisscrossed the countryside surrounding her home.

As summer eased into autumn, Georgia was finding more moments of contentment. Some days she would take a book and sit and read as Roger, now happy to leave her, bounded through the rusty leaves which lay on the ground. She began to accept invitations from her friends to go out again and slowly found herself beginning to reintegrate with the world. Her parents could see that she was recovering. Deep down Georgia knew that they longed for things to get back to normal and for her to be able to return to doing the job of which they were so proud. For Georgia, that prospect still seemed a long way away.

Chapter 3

2020

STEPHEN FELT NERVOUS about what he had to tell his son. He had discussed it with Ginny and they had agreed for the sake of Jack's wellbeing he had no alternative. He heard footsteps coming down the stairs and reached for the remote and switched off the television, standing as Jack entered the room. 'Have you got a moment, there's something I need to chat to you about. Would you like a drink?' Without waiting for a response Stephen crossed the room to the kitchen and put ice in two glasses, returning to the sideboard to pour two gin and tonics before handing one to Jack.

'I think I know what you're going to say Dad. Don't worry. I know I'm not cutting it at the newspaper.'

'It's not that, it's just that with Covid and everything it's been decided to...'

'Really Dad, it's OK. If anything it's a relief. To be honest I know I'm struggling a bit.'

Stephen took a mouthful of his drink and sat back on the sofa, relieved at his son's reaction.

*

The previous year, two days after they had returned from their holiday in Crete, Jack had joined his father on the train from the Kent countryside to London. As they got closer to the city, the carriages became more crowded and passengers were standing in the aisles. Outside, the sky was dark and rain streamed down the windows as the train labored its way towards Charing Cross, where they queued to get off before descending to the underground and continuing towards Victoria.

Jack had not known what to expect from his internship. He felt nervous as they entered the building but was put at ease by his father's assistant who had been tasked with helping Jack find his feet. A schedule had been worked out for the new intern to experience a number of areas across the newspapers and website. As he was the son of a senior executive journalist, the busy staff tried their best to make him welcome. He had always been sociable and got on well with most people. He was easy to like. Within days he had fitted into the office, the journalists were comfortable requesting his help with research and fact-checking and he was willing to do the most mundane tasks. As time went on he was occasionally asked to write captions and short items and soon his natural ability became clear. He learned quickly how to get the right angle and compose tight copy which could easily be cropped by the sub editors. He had now been caught by the writing bug.

One of the features editors recognised his talent, and began to commission him to write short pieces. He would work on them in the office and in the evening at home. The money was welcome, but the responsibility of writing to order brought with it the unwelcome uncertainties he had suffered throughout his life. He struggled with deadlines and having his stories edited, cut and rewritten. His father reassured him that this was part of the job, but he found the scrutiny and pressure played on his mind and it became increasingly hard to bear. What he had begun to think of as a future career started to look like a nightmare.

When Coronavirus gripped the country, many of the staff on the paper were told they had to work from home. He was kept on as an intern but had little or no interaction with the editors. He would get emails requesting copy with a brief and a deadline, but after he delivered the work there was no feedback. He felt pressure to hit the tight targets. Without personal contact with his mentors he felt isolated and stressed at the thought that he was unable to cope.

When he could, his father spent time trying to help. Stephen and Ginny, aware of their son's struggles with pressure, were worried that the problems he had as a child had returned. At first they had thought that in journalism he had found a career in which he could channel his talent. But it became clear that working on the staff of a publication would very soon send him into a downward spiral which would lead to depression.

Jack would shut himself in his room trying to work, but all he could do was lie on his bed, insecurities tumbling around in his head, unable to write a word. His behaviour brought back memories of when he was a schoolboy and would fall sick whenever faced with tests or examinations. During the holidays he was carefree and happy but when term time returned it brought with it the unwelcome companion of his anxiety.

Stephen checked with his junior colleagues about Jack's progress at work. They were reluctant to be honest about their reservations, but at last he managed to prise out of them that

Jack was failing to deliver copy on time, if at all. They tried to cover this up by assuring Stephen that his son's copy was good. But he knew that they were just making excuses for the failings which would make a career on the newspaper staff impossible to sustain. Stephen chided himself for putting his son in this position and knew that he needed to do something. He had been fooling himself when he had hoped that Jack's ADHD might have eased. He should have known better that the stresses of the job would be too much. But he knew Jack had a talent for writing and had wanted to encourage him to pursue that ability.

Stephen had taken it on himself to tell Jack that his internship had to end. He was determined to let him down lightly. He was pleasantly surprised when his son appeared relieved at the news. Stephen was pleased that Jack's anxiety had been allayed in the short term, but was well aware that his son would still have to discover a course to make his way in life. Although the ending of the internship had eased the pressure, his parents knew that being shut away at home, only able to go out for solitary walks once a day, would take its toll. In the evenings they would talk about how they longed to get out to the house they had so recently bought in Crete. It was all just so uncertain and difficult.

*

It was not until July 2021 that they saw a chance to visit Crete. It had been almost two years since their last visit. The Prime Minister, Boris Johnson, had heralded 'Freedom Day', when people could leave the UK without having to quarantine on their return. They would have to fill in a Passenger Locator Form online to enter Greece and wear face masks to fly, but that was a small price to pay for getting away.

Jack was excited about the prospect of going to Crete but his anticipation was tinged with apprehension. Since the first lockdown more than a year earlier, apart from occasional walks in the nearby countryside he had barely been outside. But when they left the house in the darkness to go to the airport, he began to savour the liberty of leaving the home which had imprisoned him for so long.

If anything, the journey was easier than they remembered. The airport was less crowded and the plane half empty as it appeared people were still reluctant to fly. Now over his initial misgiving, Jack was enthusiastic at the prospect of returning to Crete. He longed to go back to the time before the pandemic when he had newly graduated and his parents had bought the house in Epano Elounda.

As soon as he set foot on Crete, Jack felt a burden lifted off his shoulders. Unconsciously he dusted off his elementary Greek as he passed through passport control and they picked up the hire car. His father drove out of the airport and they opened the car windows to soak up the warmth and inhale the scent of the island they had so missed. Chatting excitedly, they pointed out things as though seeing them through new eyes. Jack could feel himself smiling and his parents too were elated to be returning to the village. As they descended the hillside towards Elounda, the sight of the bay further lifted their spirits. It glistened in the afternoon sunlight and a few boats were on the water making the crossing to and from Spinalonga. Driving along the quayside, several people smiled and waved as they passed by.

They continued up to Epano Elounda and parked the car. The path was overgrown with plants in full bloom and they had to push their way through, pulling the cases behind them. Standing in front of the house, they saw it had weathered the last years well. Turning the key and going in, they opened the shutters and Jack couldn't wait to go upstairs and unbolt the door to the terrace, letting the light illuminate the upper floor. Stepping outside, he crossed to the wall that surrounded the balcony. He looked over the terracotta roofs of the village to the olive groves rolling down the mountainside to where the light reflected off the brilliant white buildings of Elounda and the ultramarine water of the bay. He turned around and let the sun warm his back. His father stepped onto the terrace, handing him a glass of wine.

'Stelios who looks after the place for us kindly left this in the fridge when he turned the electricity and water on.' Stephen raised his glass.

'Cheers. *Yammas*. Here's to being back after all this time.'

'*Yammas*,' Jack and Ginny echoed.

Jack helped his father bring out the folding chairs. They flopped down in them, tired by the journey and relieved to be back in their village home. They were so relaxed they decided to eat out that evening in the local taverna which was only a stone's throw from the house.

It was early when they arrived at the taverna, a couple of tourists enjoying a drink at a table on the road outside. The door was propped open but inside was empty, the only sign of life the sound of traditional lyra music playing on the radio behind the counter. They took a seat.

'You're back!' A smiling, stocky man with jet black hair filled the door frame.

Stephen and Jack both rose from their chairs to be greeted with a bear hug by Alexander, the owner of the taverna, who then bent to kiss Ginny on both cheeks.

'It has been so long with this dreadful pandemic. I have missed all my friends.' He opened the tall drinks fridge and took out a carafe of raki and four glasses and put them on the table. 'Tonight we have got lamb shanks roasted with potatoes in the oven if you like, and all the usual things, but first we drink.' He poured four glasses of the fiery clear liquid, raised his glass and downed it in one. '*Eleftheria!* Freedom. It is so good to see you back at last.'

'*Eleftheria!*' Jack and his parents responded as their host returned to the fridge for a second carafe. He poured them another drink, which this time they sipped as they talked over the privations of recent times.

Alexander brought olives, tzatziki and bread to the table, which they hungrily fell upon before he served up plates loaded with the tender lamb, falling off the bone, and potatoes slow roasted in the juices, olive oil, mountain herbs and lemon. By the time they had cleared their plates they were full and exhausted after their early morning start, but Alexander would not contemplate them leaving until they had eaten some cheese pie dripping in honey accompanied by another round of raki. He would not hear of them paying the bill and it was nearly midnight by the time they escaped, promising to return soon, and wove their way up the path to their front door.

Jack got into bed and within minutes had fallen into dreamless sleep. He had forgotten to pull the curtain and awoke to the sun warming his face as it shone through the glass. For a split second he did not know where he was, but he felt more refreshed than he had for years and, fully awake, swung his legs out of bed, got up and walked onto the terrace. Already he could feel the heat of the sun on his body as he looked at the view and smiled. He walked back inside and could hear the tinkle of cups as his parents made coffee.

'I'm driving down to Elounda.' His father shouted up the stairs. 'What would you like for breakfast?'

'It's alright, Dad, I'll walk down. Give me a list of what we need and I'll pick it up. It won't take me long down the donkey track and it'll give you and mum a chance to unpack and enjoy your coffee. Just let me have a wash and I'll be off.'

Although early in the morning, it was getting hot as Jack set off down the narrow street which steepened as it passed Alexander's taverna and wove its way among the village houses, some sparkling white in the sunshine, others crumbling and abandoned, their flaking doors padlocked. Cats lazed on the tops of walls draped in bougainvillea, purple and pink, and geraniums flourished in terracotta pots and old olive oil tins. Elderly women dressed in black sat beside their doorways and offered toothless smiles as he wished them '*Kalimera*'.

The street passed under the new mountain road and through the olive groves, the cicadas striking up their rasping chorus. In the distance he could hear the tinkling of goat bells and the barking of the working dogs which herded them on the hillsides. The old road turned into a cobbled track bounded by dry stone walls beyond which water hissed through irrigation pipes beneath the olive trees. Jack had to keep his eyes on the ground to avoid turning an ankle on the uneven path before it rejoined the road above Elounda, emerging at the beautiful church surrounded by palms beside the harbour.

He stood for a moment looking out across the multi-coloured caiques moored on the quay. Fishermen were selling the last of their overnight catch to passers-by from wooden crates packed with ice. Taking it all in, Jack realised how much he had missed this place and regretted that he was only here for a fortnight. He successfully pushed the thought aside and turned his mind to his errands.

The family easily slipped into a familiar routine of visiting places and friends they had known for years. Days were spent swimming, eating in tavernas, and sitting talking, drinking and listening to music on their terrace overlooking the sea. They all relaxed, and tried not to check their phones for news of the Covid pandemic.

As their time in Crete began to come to an end, Stephen could to see a change in Jack's mood. At first he decided not to broach the subject but as it got closer to their departure, he realised that the prospect of returning to England was causing his son's unease. Ginny had noticed that Jack was slipping back into his depression and raised the subject with her husband. They decided that they should talk through Jack's concerns with him. Even if they could not find a solution to his problems they could at least be there for him.

That night they went to a taverna they loved, set back from the causeway to Kalidon, which looked out across the salt flats to the bay. They were seated beneath a large pergola, the tables surrounded by pots of plants bursting with colour and scent and the gentle sound of a fountain somewhere in the garden beyond. In the distance a fishing boat putt-puttered its way through the narrow canal and out to the Bay of Mirabello. They could make out the glow of the cigarette of the fisherman at the helm and the navigation lights marking his course seawards. Looking towards the bridge stirred a memory in Jack, one that had been forgotten in the mists of time. He pictured himself, a young boy emerging from the sea holding a coin, before he dropped it and it was lost.

That had been his first visit to this magical place, seventeen years ago, when life had been much simpler.

The evening was warm, a light breeze taking the edge off the heat. The waiter brought their order. Plates laden with sea bass grilled with herbs, olive oil and lemon juice were served with salad and baked potato for Ginny and Stephen. Jack had ordered *soutzoukakia*, large meatballs cooked in red wine and tomato sauce, spiced with cumin and garlic, on creamy mashed potato.

'Looks great, I'm starving. Do you remember the first time we came here when I was a kid?'

'And you stopped that beach inflatable from blowing away, while your dad and I were asleep on the beach just over there.' Ginny pointed. 'You were upset because you'd lost a coin or something and we came here to try and cheer you up.'

'It hasn't changed much. It's beautiful. I love it here.' Jack sighed at the thought that soon he would again be leaving it all behind.

'Why don't you stay on?' Stephen said, lifting bones of his filleted sea bass onto a side plate.

Jack looked at his father.

'Why don't you stay here for a bit? We can easily move your return flight, and there's nothing for you to rush home for. You can stay for three months.'

Jack's face fell at the reminder that he had no job and a very uncertain future.

'Your mum and I have been thinking and would like to make a suggestion.' Jack took a sip from his wine and put the glass back on the table. 'Why don't you think about becoming a freelance? We know you struggle with deadlines and the pressure of being told what to do, but you are a good writer. It's difficult to sell stories rather than pitch ideas, but it's not impossible. Why not take some time here to work through a few ideas. Maybe write something about Crete, I could always help by giving it to the travel editor on the paper. Whatever the outcome it's all experience. You can take your time and the house is all yours to enjoy.'

'It's not something I'd thought about before.' Jack let the idea sink in.

'You're such a good writer,' his mother encouraged. 'And the way things are at the moment, there's not much to come home for.'

The corners of Jack's mouth lifted into the hint of a smile as he contemplated the possibilities.

'You don't need to worry about money,' said Ginny. 'Your father and I can help out a bit until you get on your feet.' She turned to her husband who nodded. 'And without rent to pay you can live quite cheaply.'

'Thank you, I'd like that,' replied Jack. 'If I'm honest, I really wasn't looking forward to going back to England.'

Jack felt a weight lifted off his shoulders. His parents had always supported him through his struggles, and their idea could be a way forward. At the very least he would be able to put off his return to the gloom of England and, his father was right, he appeared to have a talent for writing. If he was in control of his work, maybe he could forge some sort of career doing something he loved.

At the house later, his father lit the candle lanterns on the wall surrounding the terrace. His mother poured them all a glass of wine and they sat as the late evening cooled into night and the stars shone like diamonds in the dark blue sky. They went online and managed to cancel Jack's return flight, getting a credit for him to rebook when he wanted to return. They enthusiastically discussed ideas that Jack could write about. Stephen suggested he might start off with a fairly generic colour piece about Crete. Of course it had been done many times before, but every year his and every other paper would run a similar article so it should be in with a chance of selling. Jack warmed to the idea as, although over the years they had spent many holidays on the island, he had not been to all of the major attractions. He had of course done a boat trip to Spinalonga, the old leper island in the Bay of Korfos, but had not been to the Minoan palace of Knossos, the palm beach at Vai or further afield to the Samaria Gorge among other places he had read about in guidebooks.

The evening before their departure, Stephen and Ginny's cases were packed before they walked down the lane for a last meal at Alexander's taverna. Jack was excited about the prospect of staying on and could see the sense in his parents' suggestion about writing his own articles and seeing if he could sell them. He was trying hard not to let the doubts he always harboured about his abilities creep in and scupper his ambition. He pushed any such thoughts away, determined to enjoy the last evening with his mum and dad.

Chapter 4

2021

WAVING HIS PARENTS off at the airport, Jack felt a pang of loneliness. As he pulled the hire car out onto the national highway, though, he managed to leave those thoughts behind. Heading east towards what was, for some time at least, his home, he began to cherish more and more his new-found freedom.

On the quayside in Elounda, he parked and watched families as they made their way to the town beach laden with bags, toys and other beach paraphernalia. For a moment again he felt sad at his parents' leaving. They would probably be boarding the plane right now. He let thoughts of their departure wash over him. Out in the bay a speed boat towing a pair of inflatable rings bounced the excited riders in its wake, tipping them into the sea. Smiling, he crossed the road. He would eat in tonight. Going to the butcher he bought chicken and went into the supermarket to buy salad, feta cheese and a bottle of wine.

It was late afternoon when he got back to the house. He made up the bed in the main bedroom where his parents had been sleeping and put away his few clothes in the wardrobe. Looking inside the bedside cupboard he found a grey, leather-bound album. Curious, he sat on the bed and opened it. On the first page was a picture of him with his mum and dad outside the apartment they had stayed in seventeen years earlier. He thought how young his parents were. It seemed a lifetime ago. Beneath the picture, written in pen in what Jack recognised as his mother's neat handwriting was 'Our first day on Crete'. Turning the page he saw photos of the harbour, the church in the square, boats… and then he came across a picture of a young boy who he recognised as himself. Underneath the caption written in the same elegant hand was 'Jack learns to snorkel'. Standing on the beach his younger self was grinning, holding a mask and tube in one hand, behind him the causeway leading up to the bridge and the remains of the old windmills in the background.

The recollection made him feel warm inside. He took delight in the thought of those days when he had first visited Crete. He remembered how he had learned to snorkel, the liberation of being able to dive down to the seabed with eyes wide open or swim for ever on the surface looking down at the shoals of fish. He thought of the remains of the ancient city of Olous and remembered the coin he had found and then dropped. In his mind's eye he could picture the young girl whose beach toy he had rescued.

He recalled the shy smile of the tanned, brown-eyed girl and her whispered thanks as she held her father's hand. What was it he thought had been on the tiny piece of metal he had retrieved from the sunken city? On one side had been a dolphin and on the other the image of a woman, encircled by a wreath.

He went to the fridge and filled a glass with wine, got his laptop and sat on the terrace. From there, in the distance he could see the very spot where the picture had been taken. He sat and opened the lid of his computer and clicked it on. He typed 'Olous, Elounda, Coin, Dolphin' into the search engine. At the top of the list of results was an online catalogue of ancient currency with a picture of a coin the same as he had found in a crack in the wall in the sunken city. The listing said that it was made of hammered bronze and dated from between 270 and 300

BC. He had been right. On one side was the image of a dolphin and on the other the head of a goddess, named Britomartis.

The discovery pulled him in and he was soon delving into the internet to find out more about the goddess. As with many of the Greek legends he had to sift through various interpretations before discovering the one that was likely to have been believed by the citizens of ancient Olous. He read that Britomartis was a beautiful nymph, the daughter of Zeus and Carme. Her name meant, in the Cretan dialect, sweet maiden. Born in the south of Crete, she was the Minoan goddess of hunting and the mountains. So alluring was she that King Minos himself became obsessed and pursued her across the island. To protect her virtue she threw herself into the sea near what is now Elounda. But her escape appeared thwarted when she became entangled in fishing nets. In the nick of time the fishermen spotted the goddess and cut her free, saving her from drowning and the attentions of the king. Since then, as an act of gratitude, the young nymph became the protector of sailors and cherished by all those who made their living from the sea.

Searching further he discovered that dolphins were revered in ancient Greece for protecting seafarers and guiding them home in storms. So venerated were they that to kill one of them was a capital offence.

He felt an urge to dive down again to the ancient city. He stared out from the terrace as darkness drew over the waters below. The lights came on marking the causeway, which looked as though it was hovering above the bay. A lone bell tolled in the church on the square and a dog answered its call from somewhere on the mountainside above. He heard the metal bird-shaped wind vane on the chimney creek as a breeze whispered up the hillside. He would see little of the sunken city tonight; perhaps he would take a swim there in the morning.

In his dreams he returned to that first visit to Elounda, to snorkelling and finding the coin, his sleep infused with the melancholy that it had not been just the coin he had lost that day.

He awoke, his head still foggy with his unresolved dream. He opened the door to the terrace and walked out, the tiles hot on the soles of his feet. A haze hung over the bay, the sun rising, blazing orange to burn off the last vestiges of dawn. Jack made a coffee which he hoped would clear his head. He searched the cupboards for a mask and snorkel tube, packing them in a beach bag along with a towel before heading out to the car.

He drove onto the road that skirted the sea, holidaymakers eating breakfast in the hotels and apartments on the waterfront. The heat haze had lifted and already families had staked their claims to umbrellas and sun beds on the beach. He parked on the edge of the causeway and crossed the road, laying his towel on a rock. He could smell the tang of salt in the air and stopped to listen to the water sucking and blowing at the shore. On the other side of the canal was the tiny chapel of Analipsi surrounded by a wall, where a lone fisherman sat casting a line out to sea. In the distance he saw a caique round the headland of the island of Kalidon.

He put his watch and keys into the bag and pulled out the snorkel. Teetering over the rocks, he waded out then took a deep breath and plunged into the water. As his eyes adjusted he could make out the remains of the ancient city through the clear water. He dived down again and again, swimming amongst the stone foundations where houses had once stood and along the streets and alleyways that had been the town's thoroughfares. He surfaced and floated on his back. In his imagination he pictured this town thriving, a centre of trade doing business with other Cretan city states and further abroad.

The sound of a shriek followed by laughter broke his reverie. Lifting his head he saw nearby, at anchor, the caique he had spotted earlier, two children jumping into the water from its deck. The boat was beautiful, and swung from a single anchor cast out astern. On either side of the bow he could see the boat's name, *Katerina*, the letters inscribed in gold on varnished mahogany plaques. Unflustered by the still air a Greek flag hung above the canopy, beneath which a couple sat drinking juice as they watched their children splashing in the water. Another man and a woman busied themselves aboard whilst all the time keeping an eye on their contented guests. On the side of the cabin Jack could make out a sign advertising 'Underwater Safaris, Stars and Legends Cruises' with a phone number below. He watched as the children swam, gloriously oblivious to the sunken city which lay close by on the seabed.

Jack turned his gaze from the boat. Treading water, he looked towards the shore and over the causeway at the Bay of Korfos, bounded by olive-veiled mountains. In the distance he saw Spinalonga and beyond, looking up, he could make out the turbines of a wind farm which overlooked the Cape of Aforesmenos.

He swam to shore and dried himself. Back in the car he searched on his phone to find the way to the wind farm. He sought solitude to get his thoughts together but the walk to the cape was a long climb in the heat of the day. There must be a road, otherwise how had they built and serviced the turbines? The map was unclear, but he thought a possible route might be from the village of Vrouchas which lay high above in the mountains. He put the directions into his phone and drove back to Elounda, through the square and onto the road hugging the seafront towards Plaka. From here the road rose steeply, hairpinning up the mountainside. Jack slowed the car to almost a standstill and looked out at the view of the bay below.

Before Vrouchas his phone told him to turn off the mountain road. He could see the turbines in front of him. This high up there must be some wind as the blades of the giant structures were turning slowly. Through the open car window he could hear the whirring sound as they cranked around. On the ground beneath the huge machines were solar panels, luminous in the sunlight. He brought the car to a halt at a chapel. On his phone he saw it was the Monastery of Agios Ioannis. A neatly painted church, its single bell hung in a belfry topped with a cross, and its walls reflected the midday sun. Behind it the wind turbines rotated but nearby, bent and stooped trees bore witness to the force the prevailing winds could bring to bear on this remote spot. Looking over the cliffs he could see Spinalonga standing guard of the bay.

Ahead lay a track which led to the promontory, the Cape of Aforesmenos. He left his car by the chapel and followed the winding dirt path along the cliff tops. He could feel the wind rising and see red dust blowing off the narrow path. Looking back he saw the turbines had responded and sensed the power as they rotated faster and faster. When the path approached the edge of the cliff he stopped. In front of him the land fell away hundreds of feet to the sea below. He heard the waves breaking and shivered at the rollers crashing over the rocks. There was something eerie about the old tumbledown lighthouse, its cupola long blown away, exposing the rusting rails which once surrounded the light and the gallery deck. Jack scrambled down to the doorway and stuck his head inside. The piles of stones which had once been part of the walls made him think better of going inside, and he climbed back up to the top of the cliff.

If there had been anything ghostly about the wreck of the old lighthouse, there was something about standing on this remote mountainside staring out at the infinite sea which Jack found liberating. The wind whistled past his ears as it gusted. White horses raced towards the coast before breaking and galloping over the rocks below. Further offshore the sea appeared more serene, as though the waves had been ironed into a flat sheet of ultramarine stretching away until almost imperceptibly meeting the sky.

Out to sea he allowed his eyes to focus on a line of yellow dots bouncing on the surface of the water. He took his phone from his pocket and using the camera zoomed in as close as he could. He could not see clearly, but presumed they were the floats on nets cast by fishermen. As he scanned the waters he noticed something break the surface. In a moment it had gone. He held his gaze and was rewarded by seeing one and then another creature leap clear of the water before disappearing. He kept staring around the yellow buoys but nothing revealed itself. Could they have been dolphins? His glimpse had been too brief to confirm his thoughts, but his imagination had seen enough to run with the notion and with it the hint of an idea for an article began to emerge. He put the phone back in his pocket and made his way to the path, retracing his steps to the car.

In the years he had been coming on holiday to Crete, he had not heard of dolphins being seen in and around Elounda. But the coin he had found all those years ago had a dolphin on one face. He could vaguely remember seeing dolphins depicted on the mosaic floor of the basilica of Olous, which he had visited with his parents years ago, near the chapel of Analipsi on the other side of the canal from the sunken city. He remembered his father's surprise that such an ancient monument was left uncovered and unprotected. At the time he had taken little interest. In the tourist shops you could buy dolphin fridge magnets and he was sure he had seen holiday apartments named Dolphins on the seafront. He had a vague recollection that he had seen a picture in a book of a dolphin fresco at the Minoan

Palace of Knossos near Heraklion. At least the dolphin motif might be a hook on which he could hang a feature about Elounda.

The idea of dolphins inhabited his mind as he took the track towards the wind farm. The sails were now turning fast and the noise of the turbines wove a sonorous chorus around the whistling wind. A dark cloud hung over the cliff top and Jack was pleased as the car door blew shut behind him and he started the engine and slowly began his journey down the mountain. Back on the road which curled its way from Vrouchas, the sun came back out and the view in front of him was spectacular. The bay glistened like a looking glass. He pulled the car over and got out to take a photograph. Below was the Venetian fortress of Spinalonga, which until little more than half a century before been used as a leper colony, and now had become one of Crete's most popular tourist attractions.

He felt a twinge of hunger and looked at his watch. It was already late in the afternoon, and he realised he had not eaten. The thought of food made his stomach rumble and he got back in the car and headed down the mountainside, squeezing it past the tourists in Plaka, past the luxury hotel complexes, their residents catching the last of the afternoon sun on the adjacent beaches.

Approaching Elounda, he noticed an inviting taverna near the waterfront. A sign announced it as The Boatyard, and beneath a shelter erected to one side of the building Jack could see the skeletal frame of a wooden caique under construction. To the other side was a kiosk promoting 'Underwater Safaris, Stars and Legends Cruises' – the same trips as the vessel anchored near the sunken city that morning. Looking seawards, sure enough, there was the beautiful boat called *Katerina* moored stern in to the jetty beyond the taverna.

It was still early, and he easily found a table looking out across the bay. A smiling woman approached and he wished her '*Kalispera*'.

'Good evening,' she responded in perfect English. Jack thought about continuing in his halting Greek but thought that might sound ridiculous.

'You're English?' he enquired of the woman, who handed him a menu.

'I'm Greek, but I spent much of my life working in England, and my husband is Scottish. Can I get you a drink while you decide what you want to eat?'

'I'll have a large draught beer and I think I know what I'd like to eat if you do a pork gyros with all the trimmings? I'm ravenous.'

'We certainly do,' replied the woman scribbling the order on her pad.

'Do you have anything to do with the boat tours?' Jack asked. 'The ones advertised at the kiosk outside?'

'That's my daughter Popi's business; she's a marine biologist and runs the trips with her husband Costas. I'll get you a leaflet. They'll probably be in for a drink later if you're interested in booking something up?'

'I'm a journalist,' Jack surprised himself saying. 'I'm thinking of doing an article based around Elounda and would love to talk to your daughter if she has time. Maybe you could introduce us if she comes in?'

'I'm sure she would be keen to meet you. Any publicity for the business would be welcome. I'll point her in your direction if she shows up. If not you can usually catch her early in the morning preparing the boat for sea.'

The beer arrived in a glass chilled white, icy to the touch and wet with condensation as Jack raised it to his lips and took the first sip. He looked out at the caique moored on the quay and beyond at the calm waters set against the backdrop of the scrubby hills of Kalidon. For so many years growing up this had been his happy place. If he could not write a good article about somewhere he loved so much he would never be able to write anything.

When his gyros came, Jack's hunger only just matched the plate loaded with sliced pork, pita bread, salad, chips and tzatziki. Taking a last mouthful he pushed his chair back and stretched out before taking another sip of beer. On the quay he saw a woman and a man bending down adjusting the mooring ropes of the caique before turning, taking each other's hand and walking towards the taverna.

He was tall and muscular, his long dark hair pulled into a ponytail. She was wearing shorts and a T-shirt, her arms and legs deeply tanned, laughing as she leant her head into the man's bare chest.

The woman serving him appeared, taking his empty plate. 'Did you enjoy it?' she asked.

'*Ola kala*,' Jack remembered.

'Would you like another drink?'

'*Nai. Parakalo.*'

'That's my daughter and her husband coming now. I'll tell them you'd like to chat.'

As the couple entered the taverna the woman approached them and turned to indicate where Jack was sitting. The younger woman and her husband smiled as they approached Jack's table. He stood and held out a hand.

'Hi, I'm Popi, and this is my husband Costas. My mum tells me you are writing an article and are interested in the tours?'

'Would you like a drink?' Jack asked. 'Please, sit.'

After Jack had ordered drinks for the couple he explained how he had seen their boat at anchor near the sunken city that morning and how later he thought he had spotted dolphins from the ruin of the old lighthouse high up above the Cape of Aforesmenos.

'I'm thinking of writing an article about Crete and Elounda in particular, and it occurred to me that dolphins would be a good hook for my story with them being linked to Olous and Knossos and people love dolphins.' Jack explained. 'Do you ever see them in the bay here?'

'I'm afraid not,' replied Popi. Have you ever seen them in Korfos, Costa?'

'No, they don't like the shallow waters here.' Costas spoke perfect English with a strong Cretan accent. 'We have seen them offshore on our tours and around the cape where you saw them today and far out in the Bay of Mirabello. The fishermen often talk of seeing them between the strait near Spinalonga and the cape where they sometimes raid their nets for fish and put holes in them. They are not so popular when the fishermen lose their catch and have to spend days mending their gear. So yes we do have them around, but rarely if ever in the bay itself. The dolphin population is suffering because of climate change, pollution, and the degradation of their environment. I hope that doesn't ruin your story?'

'No, I think it's enough that they are around and a modern-day link to the island's past. I remember seeing them on the mosaic of the basilica of Olous close to where you were moored today.'

'That's right, although they have covered it now to do some restoration work,' said Popi.

She looked up, and following her gaze Jack noticed a group of people standing on the jetty. 'I'm sorry, we have to go. We've got a Stars and Legends cruise booked for this evening. It's the first we've had since the end of the pandemic.' Popi stood, smiling. 'It's been good talking, I hope it's been of use. Give us a mention if you can squeeze us in to your article. We could do with all the help we can get at the moment and if you ever fancy a boat trip, you know where we are.'

'Thank you! It's been good to meet you both. You've been a great help.' Jack stood and shook their hands. 'Good luck with the cruise.' He watched as the couple walked to the end of the quay to greet their guests. Ordering another beer, he sat pondering how he would structure the piece he hoped to write. The sun was already going down. He heard the engine aboard Popi's caique come to life and the lights come on and could make out Costas helping the tourists aboard then casting off the stern line before Popi edged the boat out into the darkening waters of the bay.

*

Jack stood staring in wonder at the fresco of the two vibrant blue dolphins swimming amongst yellow, pink and blue fish against a net-patterned background. He read in his guidebook that the date the scene was painted was uncertain but thought to be around 1500 BC, during the early Neopalatial period of the Minoan civilisation.

The Archaeological Museum of Heraklion was a welcome refuge from the site of the Minoan palace itself, from where he had retreated. Although it was difficult to deny the magnificence of the reconstructed palace of Knossos, for Jack it had been impossible to think in the heat, dust and jostling summer crowds pushing their way around. There was no doubting its extraordinary scale and sophistication, but the coaches hooting their horns, guided tours and crowds of holidaymakers talking loudly in every imaginable language were distracting.

He had at least managed to get as far as the east wing, to the Queen's Megaron, the room where the original fragments of this painting had been found. With his phone he took a picture of the reproduction of the Dolphin Fresco above a doorway, then pushed his way against the tide of tourists and headed for the exit.

Now in the museum he was able to collect his thoughts. Light streamed into the air-conditioned rooms as he stood before the reconstructed original painting. In the cool and quiet of the museum, there was something calming about the picture. He wondered at the artistry of the painter who had first created the masterpiece and at the patience of the meticulous restorer who had pieced it back together from the fragments found at Knossos.

His mind drifted back to the coin. It came to him that there was a link between it and the picture, as the Minoan civilisation which so revered the dolphins had been named after Minos, the king who had pursued Britomartis. He allowed his imagination to transport him to those times and focus on what life might have been like during that remarkable Minoan period.

Chapter 5

2023

THE DARKNESS IN his head slowly cleared and as it did so the pain in his left side intensified.

Jack heard himself cry out in agony.

'He's coming round.'

'Give him some more pain relief.' The voices floated in the air for a moment before he slipped back into unconsciousness.

The next time he awoke he could feel movement. He opened his eyes. Someone held his hand and he could hear a woman speaking. She then leaned over him.

'Stay still. You are in an ambulance,' the woman spoke in heavily accented English. For a moment Jack felt the bumps of the potholed road beneath him before he fell back to sleep.

He awoke sometime later to see his father and mother by his bedside. His dad stood up and left but he felt his mother clasp his hand. He tried to speak but no words came from his mouth. Ginny held a cup of water to his lips as Stephen returned with a nurse, who began taking readings from various monitors and recording his temperature and blood pressure. She stuck some wires to his chest, pressed the button on a printer and tore off a spool of paper before studying it and leaving the room.

Some minutes later she returned with a white-coated woman. He could hear that she was talking quietly to his parents but could not make out what was being said.

The doctor bent down and spoke directly to him. 'How are you feeling?'

Jack tried, but couldn't find the words to respond.

'If it is alright with you, I would like to examine your leg.' The doctor gently pulled back the sheet and he saw his mother turn away as his father suppressed a grimace.

His mother gripped his hand again. He tried to lift his head from the bed but could not move. He felt his father's gentle hand on his shoulder.

The doctor unbound the dressing, examining the wound before redressing it. 'Everything is looking as we'd hoped it should be. It is still early days and we need to watch out for infection. We will continue with the antibiotics and pain relief but he is doing well considering the trauma he has been through.'

Jack caught just a few of the words as the doctor spoke to his parents.

'As his wounds heal, it will be how he copes with the psychological trauma as much as anything that will determine the course of his recovery. When he is fit enough to travel, is it your intention to take him back to the UK for rehabilitation?'

'Whatever is best for him, doctor? We will be guided by you,' said Stephen.

'Well, let's see how he progresses, but my advice would be to get him home. With the war here our medical resources are stretched and for his long-term recovery he would most likely get more support in your country, particularly if he is to adapt to a prosthetic limb. But in the meantime, we must get him well. You have time to consider your options.'

Jack felt a wave of pain pass through him. The doctor instructed the nurse to administer more relief and he felt himself detach from the discomfort, then descend into unconsciousness.

Each time he opened his eyes, he would see either his mother or father sitting by his bedside. Nurses and doctors came and went but Jack had no idea what had brought him to this place.

He did not know how long it was before he found his voice but knew he had when his father responded to his attempt to talk.

'Where am I?'

'You are in hospital in Kyiv.' Stephen grasped his son's hand then stood and reached for the jug of water beside the bed, poured him a drink and brought it to his lips.

'How did I get here?' The water was a welcome relief on his parched throat.

'You've had an accident. I'll tell the doctor you're awake and talking.' Jack felt his father squeeze his hand then heard him leave the room. Minutes later, Jack sensed his father return.

'Dad, what's happened to me?'

Jack heard his father take a deep breath. 'You have had your left leg amputated below the knee. You were injured in a drone attack, but other than that we have little detail. Your mother and I flew out here as soon as we received the phone call to tell us you had been hurt.'

Jack said nothing, his mind desperately trying to take in the news.

His father filled the uncomfortable silence. 'As soon as you're fit enough to travel, we'll get you home to England.'

'Thank you,' was all Jack could reply as his head whirled before he fell back into troubled sleep.

Over the following days he pieced together the events that had brought him to a hospital ward in the Ukrainian capital.

*

Jack had loved being a freelance writer. He was lucky that with the support of his parents he was able to write pieces in his own time before trying to sell them to newspapers or magazines. He knew that he could make more money if he accepted commissions, but doing speculative pieces removed the tyranny of the deadline which he so feared.

That first travel piece he had written about Crete had taken him almost three months to write before he returned home to England. It had been had been published in the newspaper his father worked for and was well received. With a certain amount of rewriting he managed to sell similar pieces to other publications and, with his byline getting known, opportunities began to open up for him. The freedom to write about what he wanted suited his evanescent attentions and without external pressures he could return again and again to his work until he was satisfied with it. He realised that he was fortunate to be able to live at home with his parents who were happy to feed him and keep a roof over his head but he enjoyed his work and as time went by, he began to get recognised for the quality of his writing.

When Russian troops invaded Ukraine in February 2022, he had watched fascinated as news anchors and foreign correspondents reported the events from the war zone on television. As those early days of the war wore on and a steady stream of refugees left the country, something attracted Jack to move in the opposite direction. He felt pulled towards the chaos and saw a chance to maybe make a living selling stories wherever he could get them on the front line.

When he first mooted the idea, his mother had been firmly against it. His father was worried about the significant risks involved, but had been reluctant to stand in the way of his son. This had been Jack's own idea and he was loath to quash it. He told himself that his newspaper had sent journalists to report on the war and, whatever the undoubted dangers, it would be hypocritical of him to veto it.

It was several months into the war before Jack could find his way to Ukraine. He managed to negotiate a lift with a van full of aid which had been collected by a local charity in Kent. By the time Jack arrived at the depot near Kyiv, the fortunes of war had waxed and waned. Initial Russian gains had been slowed or halted and a Russian advance on the capital city had turned into a humiliation as the invading troops had been forced to retreat behind their own borders. It had been in the winter of the first year of the conflict that Jack arrived and the war had got bogged down in the grinding wet and cold.

He spent his time in the hotels and bars of the capital, mixing with journalists of all nationalities, making contacts and taking the opportunity to write background and colour pieces which he sent home to features editors hungry to publish stories from the conflict. As winter turned to spring, rumours began to emerge about a counter offensive by the Ukrainian army in the east of the country in the regions of Donetsk, Zaporizihzhia and Kherson. Jack was eager to get close to the action and spent much of the spring months seeking the permissions he would need to report on the fighting near the front line.

The first opportunity he got was to join a squad backing up an assault brigade tasked with capturing Klishchiivka and the neighbouring village of Andriivka. Progress was slow but the Ukrainian forces pushed the Russian troops back. The retreat was covered by heavy artillery fire and drone attacks as the brigade fought its way across open fields strewn with craters and minefields.

It was early September when Jack's life was changed forever. His squad was carefully navigating a path marked through a minefield swept by the advancing assault brigade when they were attacked by an armed drone. The grenade hit the ground some metres from Jack, but the force of the explosion was enough to critically injure his left leg. That was the last thing he remembered. He knew nothing of how he had been given emergency first aid to stem the bleeding in his shattered leg or of the journey back to the makeshift field hospital where surgeons operated to amputate his limb before he was taken by ambulance to a hospital 500 miles away in Kyiv.

*

Over the following weeks Jack worked hard on his rehabilitation. His physiotherapy concentrated on him being able to transfer himself into a wheelchair, walking on crutches and getting fit to travel back to the UK, where the intention was to get a prosthetic fitted and continue his physical and psychological rehabilitation. Ginny remained with her son in Kyiv, while Stephen returned to do some work and arrange for the modifications needed to accommodate Jack at home, before taking the drive back to Ukraine to transport him to England.

With Jack coming to terms with the loss of his leg, he surprised himself with how he managed to focus on his recovery. Rather than worry that he was not working hard enough to build up his strength, sometimes the medical staff had to stop him from doing too much for fear of exhaustion. As the wound healed, his other leg grew stronger along with his arms. He was determined that he would walk again as soon as possible and adapt to his new normality.

They were all keen to get the journey over as quickly as possible, so Ginny and Stephen decided to share the driving, hoping that they could cover the 1,500-mile trip from Ukraine through Poland, Germany, Belgium and France to the Channel Tunnel in less than two days. Jack was excited to be going home at last and at the challenge of rebuilding his life. As they sped past Warsaw and Berlin he felt his mood lift. His parents were also keen to get the journey over and done with, only stopping to eat and fill up with fuel.

As they drove onto the train near Calais, Jack could tell his parents were exhausted but they were all relieved that the ordeal was nearly over. When they emerged from the tunnel in Folkestone they were little more than an hour's journey from home. Jack looked out of the car window at the neat patchwork of fields. Even the slight drizzle on the windscreen could not dampen the gratitude he felt to be home, and to be alive.

Stephen had turned his home office into a downstairs bedroom so that Jack did not have to struggle with the stairs, and had moved his son's books, clothes and other possessions into the room.

The following weeks were taken up with appointments with the GP, hospital consultants and the prosthetist, who hoped, as Jack's wound was already healed, that he could be fitted with a prosthetic before Christmas. Jack was still frustrated by the time it took. After the leg had been made, the prosthetist was meticulous in ensuring the fit of the socket was comfortable. It was finished in the week before Christmas, but the doctors were insistent that he wait until the New Year before using it. He needed the attentions of a therapist to help adjust to using his prosthetic, to improve his strength, balance and coordination.

Although disappointed that he was unable to use his new leg, Jack was persuaded by his father that it was best to be patient rather than risk a setback to his recovery. The diversions of Christmas went some way to quelling his upset at the delay. He ordered presents for his parents on the internet and sat at the dining table wrapping them. He went to the local pub and met up with old school friends who had returned home to their families in the village for Christmas. Balancing on his crutches, he insisted on helping his parents decorate the Christmas tree and even managed to reach up to place the angel on the top.

Jack had always felt a sense of melancholy when Christmas was over, and in the days following the big event, his mood began to sink. He desperately needed something on which to focus his attention and energy. In his darker moments he regretted his decision to go to Ukraine but he could still feel the excitement of the danger and the satisfaction he had got from selling his stories to the newspapers back home. He knew that he needed a challenge and at the moment that was to get walking. The delay to his rehabilitation was torturous.

If the days following Christmas had been difficult, then New Year's Eve was miserable. He had always hated the close of the year. His head could never focus on much other than the bleak prospect of the months of January and February stretching out in front of him. His parents had gone out to a party at a neighbours' and Jack woke up, an empty bottle of wine beside him, to the strains of 'Auld Lang Syne' coming from the TV.

He made his way to bed, falling asleep almost immediately, not waking until he heard a knock on the door, as his mother came in bringing him a cup of coffee and wishing him 'Happy New Year'. Against the window he could hear the rain lashing. He crossed the room and lifted the curtain before letting it drop back and returning to bed to have his drink. He considered trying to go back to sleep but knew this would only make facing the day harder. He washed and cleaned his teeth and was cheered as he entered the open plan kitchen living room to see a fire burning in the grate.

'Grab a seat at the table; I'll cook your eggs.' His father stood beside the stove and within minutes breakfast was in front of Jack. He surprised himself with how hungry he felt, and the food lifted his mood.

'Would you like more tea?' Stephen picked up his wife's mug from the table. 'I'll get you another coffee,' he said to Jack.

Placing the two drinks down on the table, Stephen sat. 'Your mother and I have got you a little present. We know how much you love New Year,' he smiled. 'We thought it might cheer you up.'

His mother lifted a gift bag up from beside her chair and put it on the table in front of Jack. Inside was a box. He lifted the lid and took out an album. Opening it he saw that carefully mounted on each page were copies of every story he had had published, from his early days as an intern at his father's newspaper to his travel pieces on Crete and his features from the war in Ukraine. The album was not even half full, but already represented a significant body of work.

His parents remained silent as Jack turned the pages slowly, as though taking in for the first time what he had achieved over the last few years.

'Thank you, I never thought to keep them myself,' was all he could think of to say, sensing a warm feeling pass through him.

'And there are plenty of blank pages left in the book for you to put your next work in.' His mother looked at him, smiling. 'You might not be returning to a war zone, but the world is a big place and there is so much you can write about. Can't you see how much the newspapers and magazines love your work?'

Jack hoisted himself onto his crutches and crossed the room to where his mother sat and gave her an unsteady hug.

Ginny continued. 'It's only two days before you go to the hospital and can start getting used to your new leg. Then there will be no stopping you.' She squeezed him tight and Jack felt a tear come to his eye.

'Thanks Mum, thanks Dad. I know I don't always show it but I appreciate everything you've done for me. Even before all this happened.'

'We're very proud of all that you've achieved,' his father said. 'We've done only what most parents would do. I'd suggest we go for a walk but it's apocalyptic out there. How about you two relax whilst I cook us a casserole for later?'

Jack and Ginny moved from the table to sit on the chairs around the open fire, where his mother picked up her book and Jack flicked through the pages of the cuttings album. He allowed himself the indulgence of reading the pieces he had written and could tell how his work had progressed since those first features he had done as an intern. In the travel pieces he could now sense the love which he held for Crete and in his more recent reporting from Ukraine, a desire to present to readers the full horrors of the war. He knew that his parents had given him the book to jog him into thinking there was still a career for him in writing. He was grateful for that because in moments like this he could see a future despite his disability. But he knew that there would be plenty of dark times. Even before his traumatic injury, Jack had struggled with anxiety; he had got better at managing his mental health as he had got older but was aware that his recent impairment would make things more difficult. Still, for the time being he felt positive and would hold on to that for as long as he could.

*

The day Jack was to have his prosthetic fitted, he was awake early. Opening the curtains it was barely light, but even the brooding winter obscurity could not diminish Jack's excitement at the thought of what lay ahead. He had not slept well, buzzing with the anticipation of how the day would be the start of his new life.

Before his appointment with the prosthetist he had a consultation with a doctor who explained any complications which could arise. 'You have been through a huge trauma,' the consultant said. 'The road to recovery can be bumpy psychologically as well as physically. If you get any problems with your mental health, go to your GP, who will refer you to a clinical psychologist.' Any physical problems that occurred while he was working with the physiotherapist would be dealt with at the hospital. 'If you have any problems after you are discharged, ask your doctor to refer you back to me.'

Jack appreciated the doctor was doing his job but was anxious to get his new leg. Eventually he was ushered in to see the prosthetist and felt a rising frustration as he checked again the exact fit of the leg before describing how he should care for it. Jack knew he was being impatient and tried to calm his thoughts until eventually he was taken to see the physiotherapist. She explained the fundamentals of using the prosthetic before announcing, 'I think the best thing we can do is to give it a go. If it's comfortable and you manage to take a few steps, you'll be able to take it home with you today.'

Since leaving Ukraine he had worked hard on the fitness regime he had been given by the medical staff to prepare himself. Resolved to regain his independence, he summoned all his willpower to stand up unaided, then to walk a short distance, even climbing a few steps. The physiotherapist was concerned that he was overstretching himself but was happy with his progress, and he was allowed to take his prosthetic home.

Each time he returned to the hospital to see the physio, she was impressed with Jack's determination. In little more than a week of having his new leg he persuaded his parents to move his bedroom back to the first floor so that he got more practice climbing up and down the staircase. Within a month, he was beginning to look at the possibility of driving. He thought that with the right car he would be able to do it, and after an assessment he was granted a licence for an automatic vehicle. Realising the boost being able to drive again would give their son, his parents agreed to buy him a car and Jack began to scour the internet to find one suitable.

On the day he saw the first blossom on the cherry tree outside his bedroom window, he was discharged from the hospital's care. At first he was elated by the progress he had made but, as the days went by and the pink petals had been strewn around the lawn by the April winds, he began to feel the void left by no longer having to push himself to learn to walk with his new leg. With the loss of the challenge he had posed himself, he now felt his mood begin to sink into the old, familiar anxiety. He could not help but feel the irony.

He knew he needed to work. His parents had been generous both with their time and supporting him, and although they assured him they would always be there to help, he felt guilty that he was a burden. He tried to write about losing his leg in Ukraine, but the memories were too painful. Whenever he tried to put his experiences down on paper he felt himself sliding into a frightening depression. Not working, he despaired at his inactivity, but somehow could not find the mental strength to change his direction. He went to see his GP to get a referral for counselling, but the waiting list was more than six months.

He found himself drifting, eating erratically and putting on weight. He would sit up late into the evening watching TV and drinking wine, very often falling asleep in a chair. Even as spring began to herald summer, and the days grew brighter and longer, he withdrew into himself, going outside the front door less and less. His parents offered to pay for counselling, but he steadfastly refused. The more his anxiety played on his mind, the less he wanted to talk about it. It would come and go in waves and in his calmer moments he would go on the internet and seek out videos that might help him. Often he knew that the advice they gave was what he needed but then he would descend into a state of fretfulness that rendered taking any action impossible.

His parents could see that their son's mental health was deteriorating, but Jack's stubborn refusal to accept their offer to pay for help left them impotent. Stephen was not prepared to let the matter lie, and began to research ways in which he might help his son. He found on the internet a charitable fund for journalists to seek treatment for trauma issues. Perhaps he could persuade Jack to apply to them for help?

Chapter 6

2024

THE WATER WAS gloriously cold and the sand squeezed up between her toes. The sun had not long risen and Georgia was pleased she had made an early start to avoid the crowds. Rather than await the morning ferry, she had booked a water taxi for the trip along the coast from Paleochora to the beach at Elafonisi. Setting off as dawn broke, the journey along the rugged coastline had been magical.

The sea was the very definition of turquoise and through its lens the smooth sand beneath was tinged with the pinks and reds of tiny shells which had eroded over the centuries. Behind her a few early sun worshippers lay under umbrellas. She continued to wade towards the island across the natural causeway created by a sandbank.

The sunshine warmed her shoulders and lifted her spirits as she pushed forwards towards the island of Elafonisi. She bent down to wet a hand and rubbed the cool water over the back of her neck. As a child she had loved coming here. She tried to think when it was that she had last visited and realised it must have been as a teenager, before the world had become serious. Since then her grandfather had died, the year before she went to university. She had travelled with her parents for the funeral, but had not set foot on Crete since, until now. She realised she had missed it sorely. She noted there were now more sun beds on the beach and she could not remember camper vans parked on the sand back then. She quickly turned and continued her walk towards the deserted island.

Her grandmother, Maria, had been delighted when Georgia had phoned to ask if she could come and stay, even more so since the length of her visit was unspecified. Maria had embraced life stoically since her husband's death and now, in her eightieth year, remained positive and cheerful but, Georgia thought, sometimes must have felt lonely.

Being with her *yiayia* gave Georgia strength. Born in the last days of the Second World War, her grandmother had not had an easy life. Maria's parents had had to work hard to secure a living from their meagre plot of land after the occupation. The threat of violence was never far away as Crete was gripped by the civil war which raged throughout Greece. Despite those hardships, her grandmother looked back fondly on her childhood. She was still just a girl when she left school to help her mother around the home and her father on their smallholding in the hills.

Maria's marriage had been arranged when she was seventeen but somehow she had made it work and looked back on the years up until her husband's death with great affection. Despite the privations of the days of the military Junta, Maria and her husband had worked hard, sacrificing everything to provide their only child with an education. They were beyond proud when he qualified as a doctor. When Nikos had moved to England his parents had supported his decision, although deep down Maria missed him terribly. She was delighted when her son announced he was getting married to Christine, and after Georgia was born she could hardly contain herself as the time approached when they would visit for holidays.

Georgia stepped out of the shallow water and felt the thrill of being alone, the only person on the empty island. Later in the day it would be busy, but for now she had this remote corner of south-western Crete to herself. She sat on the sand and pulled up her dress to let the sun dry her legs. At moments like these she knew she was making progress on her long road to recovery. The incidents of darkness were getting less and less, but she knew from experience that they could still sneak up on her at any time.

Although Georgia was a long way away from the crisis she had suffered, she was aware that she harboured guilt at not feeling able to pursue a career as a doctor and believed that her instability would make it impossible for her to find love. She could see no way that she could find a partner, let alone sustain a relationship. She longed to have a child but that could never happen. She felt too fragile, her confidence at rock bottom.

Her psychologist had agreed that a trip to Crete might help. She had to admit that since arriving a week earlier she had been more positive, spending her days in the mountains, walking by the sea or through the shady streets in Paleochora.

Taking her shoes from her pack, she brushed the sand from her feet and put them on. She walked off the beach between the roots of waxy smelling rock samphire, white and green false dittany and Mediterranean saltbushes. A short track led her to the highest point on the low-lying island. She looked out over the Libyan Sea, then back at the lagoon. It felt like she was on the edge of the world.

Georgia descended to the beach at the seaward side of island and lay down on the sand. She could hear nothing but the ripples of the water sighing at the shoreline. She closed her eyes and allowed herself the joy of living in that moment before the spell was broken when a wave came up the beach and washed over her toes. She sat up and saw a passing ship heading south for Africa. She lay down again but could not regain the calm. Unwanted thoughts invaded her head. She tried to reach for the coping mechanisms taught by her therapist. She managed to let the tide of adversity flow over her but knew that for now the moment of tranquillity had deserted her.

She took a band from her wrist and swept back her hair, tying it into a bunch. Pulling her sun dress over her head, she put it beneath her back pack. At first the sea was chilly. She waded in knee deep, bending to splash water over her dark blue swimming costume. Taking the plunge, she swam out into deeper water. The cold rinsed any negative thoughts from her head. As her body acclimatised she rolled onto her back and floated on the salty cushion that embraced her. If only life could always be like this?

She lay on the sand, allowing the sun to dry her. Already she could hear the chatter of the first tourists arriving on the secluded beach. She pulled her dress over the damp swimming costume and walked against the tide of day trippers towards the sand bar.

On the main beach most of the sun beds were occupied. Kite surfers, paddle boarders and kayakers had already taken to the water. Georgia continued walking until the sand gave way to rocks and picked her way along the coast to where she saw a ferry discharging its passengers onto a quay. The boat would be returning to Paleochora empty, and the captain recognised Georgia, knowing her grandmother, and agreed to take her back to town.

The early start, walking and sea air had left Georgia famished. She persuaded her grandmother to join her for lunch at a taverna on the less busy side of the promontory on which the town sat. The first blooms of bougainvillea tumbled from balconies, and geraniums of every colour burst from containers in the alleyways off which arched doorways revealed tantalising glimpses of shaded courtyards. The taverna looked out across a beach and the sea stretching westward across which Georgia had sailed that morning.

Both women ordered the roast knuckle of pork served with potatoes. The meat just fell from the bone and the herby potatoes tasted of lemon and olive oil. They were too full to eat a dessert, but the waiter brought a plate of apricots, figs and strawberries and a karafaki of raki. Georgia loved her *yiayia*, who had doted on her since she was a baby. She did not dress in widow's weeds. She had not even worn black to her husband's funeral.

Georgia found that she could talk to her *yiayia* in a way she could not with her mother and father. That afternoon, they lingered over the raki. Maria listened as her granddaughter opened up about her anxiety, depression and breakdown and her worry about the toll these things had taken on her life. She was a good listener and let Georgia talk.

'You must be patient and give yourself time,' Maria said as she leaned across the table and took Georgia's hand. 'You must show yourself the same compassion you would show others. If you are kind to yourself it will help you get better. The island will give you a helping hand, believe me.'

*

Georgia took her *yiayia's* advice and began to relax into the Cretan way of life. She gave herself time to enjoy the beauty that surrounded her and the simple pleasures of eating and having long chats with her grandmother. Those early days she did not stray from the south-west corner of the island, but as she felt herself grow stronger, she began to go further afield.

At first she had been nervous about going to Chania, but her grandmother had a doctor's appointment there, and Georgia thought it was only right that she accompany her. The clinic was close to the bus station and Maria insisted that Georgia was not to wait but to meet her in a café opposite in two hours' time. The younger woman sensed that she was being manipulated into confronting her fear of the busy streets but felt strong enough to acquiesce. Her grandmother had been right so far about the island helping her regain equilibrium and she had grown to trust Maria's instincts.

She set out through the narrow streets of the old town, feeling a hint of anxiety tiptoeing up and tugging at her sleeve. She shrugged it off, diverting her attentions to the faded grandeur of the Venetian and Turkish buildings, their balconies bursting with flowers of every colour. Georgia could not help but smile.

She emerged at the harbour, tavernas and cafés jostling for space along the waterfront. To her right a pink-domed mosque dominated a square looking across the water to the Venetian lighthouse at the end of the harbour wall. A horse-drawn carriage waited for customers in the *plateia* and Georgia laughed to see the horse was wearing a hat. Something drew her to the lighthouse. She set off along the front until she reached the old harbour, where pleasure boats advertising sailing cruises, sightseeing and fishing trips were moored among the traditional caiques. Passing the Venetian guardhouse, she headed out along the sea wall. The walk was further than she thought. At the lighthouse she stopped and delved into her backpack for a bottle of water and her phone to take some pictures. She was disappointed that the inside of the tower was not open to visitors but nevertheless the view from the end of the harbour wall was magnificent. Looking back at the old town, she could see the mosque and the sun reflecting off the pastel-coloured buildings which hugged the waterfront. Beyond the city she could make out the shadows of the mountains inland rising imperiously into the azure sky.

Georgia looked at her watch. She would have to walk quickly if she was going to be on time to meet her *yiayia*. When she arrived at the café her grandmother was sitting contentedly drinking a coffee. 'You look hot, sit down and have something to drink. You needn't have rushed, I am more than happy here watching the world go by.' Maria looked for the waiter and caught his eye, and he crossed to the table and took the order.

On the way home, her grandmother slept as the bus made its way west along the coast revealing tantalising glimpses of the sea before turning inland. As far as the eye could see the landscape flourished with olive groves, vineyards and orchards of chestnuts. Georgia allowed her mind to wander and it was only then she realised what she had achieved that day. She had managed to go to a crowded city and walk about on her own without being anxious. She allowed herself to feel elated but then grew wary that her happiness might only be short-lived. She let that thought pass and, taking her grandmother's hand as they got off the bus in Paleochora, began to feel more positive about the future.

Her grandmother's house lay near the beach to the west. Georgia could see that her *yiayia* was tired and insisted they take a taxi home. Minutes later they were turning onto the pebble drive.

'Oh good,' Georgia heard Maria mutter as they approached. She helped her grandmother out of the taxi and paid the fare. 'That'll do nicely,' her grandmother said to herself. Georgia's eyes followed her gaze which alighted on a car parked to the side of the house. She had not taken much notice of it before, but now something was different; before the car had been covered in red dust, its tyres deflated and hubcaps missing. Now it shone white, the sun glistening off the chrome which adorned the new wheels.

Georgia looked questioningly at her grandmother, who opened the door on the driver's side, bent down and took a key from beneath the mat, before handing it to her.

'It's all yours.' Maria smiled. 'The car was your grandfather's. He would have wanted you to have it. I can no longer drive with my eyesight so I asked Michalis from the garage to come and give it a service and tidy it up a bit. Let's try it out.' Before Georgia could reply, the elderly woman was in the passenger seat.

There was nothing else for it but for Georgia to get in. She had not driven since her breakdown and could feel herself shaking as she put the key into the ignition.

'Have a go here on the drive, see how you get on before going on the road.' Maria sensed her granddaughter's reluctance. 'You'll be fine.'

Hesitatingly Georgia took her foot off the clutch and the car crept forward. She was concentrating so much that she hadn't time to think of anything but driving. She brought the vehicle to a halt at the road which ran alongside the seafront.

'It's very quiet along here,' said Maria. 'Why not give it a go?'

No cars passed from either direction. Georgia took a deep breath, moved forward and turned left. At first she gripped the steering wheel tightly, leaning forward in her seat. It had been more than two years since she had driven. The road remained empty and gradually she sat back, relaxing her grip, even allowing her arm to rest out of the open window. Much to Georgia's amazement she realised that she had not forgotten how to drive.

At her grandmother's suggestion she found somewhere she could turn the car around and headed towards Paleochora. At first she was nervous encountering traffic, but within minutes her nerves had turned to a sense of pride at what she had achieved.

That day had worked wonders for her confidence. Back at the house, as they got out of the car, Georgia hugged her grandmother tight. 'Thank you so much, I love the car. Are you sure you don't want to sell it?'

'What need have I for the money?' Maria asked. 'Anyway, it will help me if you could drive me if I have to go into town or even to Chania like today. I'm finding I get more tired these days if I have to walk a long way. And it will be good for you to get about, maybe see a bit more of the island?'

*

Her grandmother was right, and in the days that followed she felt liberated at the opportunities being able to drive opened up. She was mindful to always ask her grandmother to accompany her. Sometimes she was taken up on the offer, and Georgia noticed that getting out and about more gave her grandmother a new lease of life.

It was Maria who suggested the two of them visit the capital city of Heraklion. Georgia was surprised to hear that her grandmother had not visited there for many years, and had never been to Knossos or the Archaeological Museum, both places she wanted to visit. It was a long way, so Georgia decided to treat them both to a hotel for two nights so they could make the most of their visit. She found one on the internet that was by the sea outside the city centre.

The day before they were due to leave, Maria was packed and her case waiting by the front door before lunch. She was like a young girl, giddy with the thrill of going on holiday. Georgia too was awash with anticipation which fluctuated between excitement and anxiety. It would be the longest distance she had driven since she had been given the car.

The following morning they set off as the sun was rising. At a bakery in Paleohora they stopped and bought *spanakopita*, the delicious parcels of filo pastry stuffed with spinach and feta cheese still warm from the oven, and flaky croissants oozing with dark chocolate. Maria tore open the paper bags and spread the breakfast on her lap, feeding her granddaughter as she drove.

As the sun rose over the mountains the air was redolent with sage, thyme and adventure.

They passed through villages, men in the traditional dress of breeches tucked into their long *stivania* boots, some sporting the fringed *saraki* kerchiefs on their heads, sitting outside the kafenio drinking Greek coffee and raki. The sun was already burnishing the silver water of the coast as they joined the national highway heading east, first past Chania, then Souda Bay and onwards to Rethymnon. Many places they would have liked to stop, but both were keen to get the journey behind them and relax.

They arrived by lunchtime and although they were early, their room was ready. Maria took a childlike joy in seeing the complimentary shampoos, shower gels and body lotion, and insisted on using the drinks-making facilities. Sitting on the balcony they could watch people on the beach and swimmers in the sea as they sat drinking coffee and nibbling biscuits.

'I don't know about you, but I'm famished after that early start. Shall we go into Heraklion and find somewhere to eat?' Maria asked.

Georgia could tell that her grandmother was eager to get out into the city she had not visited for so many years. 'I'm hungry too. I'll phone reception and ask them to order us a taxi.'

Twenty minutes later they were on their way, and ahead they could make out the fortress at the entrance to the old port. Maria asked the driver to drop them near the quayside. An onshore breeze had blown up and waves broke over the sea wall. Groups of children laughed as they dodged the cooling spray. In the calm of the harbour, fishermen sat smoking on the waterfront.

Maria took on the role of tour guide. She pointed out the arches of the Venetian Arsenals, leading her granddaughter across the road. 'This has all changed.' Maria looked around trying to get her bearings. 'The road here used to be jammed with traffic, smelly and noisy. It's much nicer now.' The thoroughfare into the city had been pedestrianised and was now a quieter, safer route for people walking up the hill towards the centre. It was the hill that concerned Georgia, but her *yiayia* seemed energised and determined to take the walk up 25 August Street. They linked arms and Georgia was not sure who was leading who as they set off past the souvenir shops, shipping agents, car rental showrooms, banks and tavernas which lined the historic road.

As they went, Maria pointed out the domed, cream stone church of St Titus, set back in its own square, shaded by palm trees. Her commentary continued as they stopped to admire the Palladian splendour of the Venetian Loggia, and St Mark's

Basilica which housed the city's art collection. On the other side of the street, a tranquil fountain guarded a square sheltered by trees and surrounded by cafés whose chairs and tables spilled out onto the *plateia*.

Maria proudly explained that the square where they stood was named after Eleftherios Venizelos, who had come from the west of the island and been instrumental in securing Crete's independence, and went on to become prime minister of Greece in 1910. Despite this, locals and tourists alike called it Lion Square after the sculpted beasts of the fountain, their mouths spouting water which cascaded into the pool beneath.

Georgia would have happily stopped there for lunch, but her grandmother was keen to continue. Negotiating a road jammed with angry traffic they crossed into a market, the narrow street lined on either side with stalls selling all manner of produce: fruit and vegetables, meat, cheese herbs, spices, oil, honey, wine and raki. The shops that lurked behind the colourful displays were dark caves stuffed with all the necessities required for everyday life.

The calls of the vendors and the smells of the produce were intoxicating. Some distance along the market Maria found what she was looking for. At an intersection, another narrow street was home to what Georgia's nose informed her was a fish market. As they turned the corner, her eyes confirmed it. Beneath the balconies of the crumbling old buildings, boxes of fish packed in ice were displayed. In the street, stall holders in aprons wheeled barrows of crates to the vans of taverna owners or gutted fish to order for the passing trade.

In the midst of the market was a taverna, some tables and chairs outside.

'Good, it's still here,' Maria remarked as she took a seat, indicating for Georgia to follow. 'I haven't been here for... well, it must be thirty years now!'

'Welcome back.' An elderly waiter with an exuberant moustache which belied the gentleness of his voice approached. 'It is good to see you again. Your husband?' He raised an eyebrow as he asked.

'Unfortunately he passed.' Maria looked down.

'May his memory be eternal. I'm sorry, my condolences.' The waiter put his hand on her shoulder.

'Thank you. He died eleven years ago. This is my granddaughter. She's a doctor.' Maria looked across the table, immediately regretting her words as she saw Georgia's face fall before regaining its composure.

'You must be very proud,' said the waiter as he handed them menus. 'What would you like to drink?'

'A small carafe of white wine?' She looked across at Georgia who nodded.

'That would be great.'

'It always amazes me how waiters remember you from so long ago, particularly when myself and your granddad had only been here two or three times.'

'It's incredible,' agreed Georgia, 'but lovely. It must make you feel really welcome.'

The waiter brought the wine and two glasses before taking their order of grilled sea bass for Maria and deep-fried calamari for Georgia. The older woman was relieved to see that her granddaughter had forgotten her faux pas. How could she have been so insensitive? But it was difficult when she was so proud of Georgia's achievements.

'What would you like to do after lunch?' asked Georgia, smiling. She thought her *yiayia* might be worried that she had upset her.

'Shall we go to the Archaeological Museum? It's ridiculous that I haven't been before. Some people travel right across the world to see it! They spent millions renovating it too. I've read it's quite something. If we are going to Knossos tomorrow in the car you won't want to drive back into the city to go then. It's not far from here.'

'What a good idea.' Georgia was keen to see the famous museum. 'I really wasn't looking forward to driving in the city centre and the parking looks a nightmare. I can't wait to see what they've got there, and that will give us more time to explore Knossos tomorrow.'

It was not far from the taverna, but after their substantial lunch and the walk there in the afternoon sun, they were grateful of the cool air-conditioned interior. The museum was on a scale that did not overwhelm but was crammed with the most impressive collection of Minoan art and artifacts in the world. Georgia and Maria were keen to see the famed figures of the Bull Leaper and Snake Goddess found in the Palace of Knossos and the much vaunted Phaistos Disc, named after the ancient palace where it was unearthed. Maria was happy that at last she had got to see the plate-sized clay dish that was famously known as the first example of moveable type in the world. She had seen replicas of it in souvenir shops but marvelled at standing so close to the real thing, although if truth be told she had expected it to be larger.

Maria was determined to make the most of her visit, but despite her protestations, Georgia could see that her grandmother was flagging. They made their way to the first floor which was quieter and found a place to sit in a long, light room, its walls covered with frescoes.

Sitting beside Maria, Georgia scanned the room. She wondered at the patience of the restorers of these ancient treasures. One in particular caught her eye. Between a frieze depicting partridges and a fragment of a painting of a young woman, which on approaching she read was called 'La Parisienne', was a beautiful fresco depicting dolphins painted in vibrant blue and yellow pigments. It was uplifting and made Georgia smile. She felt a touch of envy for the freedom of the creatures in the extraordinary picture, and something in the scene stirred a vague memory. She sat down in front of the painting and read that the fragments that had been painstakingly put back together had been found in the Queen's Apartment at Knossos. A replica of what now was in front of her had been painted on the wall above the door in the reconstruction of that room in the Minoan palace. She must have seen it in a guidebook somewhere.

Returning to Maria, she recalled a picture of herself as a child, looking at a mosaic of dolphins near a chapel looking out across a bay. With her were her father and mother. For a moment she was filled with happiness and then sadness at the thought of the joy she had lost along the way. She delved further into her thoughts and recalled on that day they had visited an island where lepers had once been confined, and then gone to a beach near a sunken city, close to the mosaic.

*

The following morning Georgia wasn't looking forward to the crowds she had heard were always swarming Knossos, generated by its reputation as a must-see destination, and despite setting off early she discovered that the rumours were sadly true. Before the gates were open, the car parks were full of squealing coaches honking their horns and belching exhaust fumes and passengers. But Maria minded not the slightest; she appeared to enjoy the hustle and bustle of standing in the queue, striking up conversations with strangers.

Once inside, Maria was like a child in a theme park, showing a surprising turn of speed as she walked between the restored buildings of the palace, and Georgia followed. With more than a thousand rooms laid out before them, it was hard not to be impressed. Georgia passed her phone to her grandmother to take a photograph in front of the familiar three red columns framing a fresco of a bull which she had seen reproduced on postcards for sale all over the island.

She pondered how the painting was a significantly enhanced copy of the original which she had seen the previous day in the museum. Why she felt uncomfortable with these enhancements she wasn't sure. But when she followed Maria into the Queen's Chamber and stood before the painting of the dolphins she had so admired in the museum, she knew it stood no comparison with the original.

On the way back to the hotel, Maria snored in the passenger seat and, as they sat in a traffic jam on the outskirts of Heraklion, Georgia noted how comfortable she felt driving. As she crawled forward she tried to rid herself of the thought in case it jinxed her wellbeing. She looked at her grandmother and smiled. She had had a good day.

Chapter 7

2024

AS THE SPRING days lengthened into summer, Georgia realised she was mending. The thought gave her hope although she was aware of the fragility which lay beneath her new-found confidence. Her grandmother had been right. The island was helping her to find some of the resilience she once had. There was no doubt that being out in the fresh air had contributed to her healing but her savings were running low and it would be unfair to expect her grandmother and parents, however willing they were, to support her indefinitely. More than that, just being able to deal with the anxiety which had brought her to her knees was not enough. She longed to return to being able to stand on her own feet and create a life which fulfilled her innermost needs.

Following the visit to Heraklion, Maria encouraged her granddaughter to take more trips out. They went to the beautiful city of Rethymnon, and Georgia even returned to Chania, this time alone. These forays bolstered her confidence and Georgia realised if she planned them well in advance she was less likely to back out.

It was her *yiayia* who suggested she visit Samaria. 'It's the longest gorge in Europe. It would be a shame not to see it when it is so close.'

Georgia had heard about the trek, and something about taking on the challenge appealed to her. When she researched the walk, however, she found the prospect of taking on the more-than-ten-mile hike in the heat of the June sunshine daunting.

'Why don't you take what they call the Lazy Way,' suggested Maria. 'You walk halfway up the gorge from the bottom and then back down. You get the early ferry from here and catch it back again in the afternoon.'

To Georgia it didn't sound that 'lazy', but she told herself the challenge would do her good. Maria suggested she grasp the nettle and accompanied her granddaughter to town that evening to book the excursion.

Two days later Georgia was on the quayside in Paleochora with a small group and tour guide awaiting the ferry to take them east along the coast to the village of Agia Roumeli. After pleasantries had passed between them, Georgia stood aside and watched as the boat edged towards the jetty, lowering the ramp as it approached.

She followed the group aboard, leaving them to go and get coffee as she went up on deck. The ship pulled away from the dock and Georgia watched it draw a circle with its wake on the water. At the rail she stood transfixed by the mountainous coastline dotted with isolated coves. Looking back she could see Paleochora sparkling in the morning sunshine, its buildings like cubes of sugar scattered on the sea shore. Georgia reached in her pack and took out a map. Unfolding it, she traced their course along the shoreline with her finger. She felt the boat turn landwards in the shadow of the sheer cliffs. Sougia's harbour was too modest even for the small ferry which docked bow first to a concrete pier jutting out into the open water. Two people with rucksacks disembarked and five more hikers equipped with walking poles ascended the ramp.

With practiced efficiency, the ferry shed its mooring. Resuming its voyage east, they passed the long pebble beach of Sougia, behind which she could make out the sleepy village which lay in the shade of the towering mountains. She looked at her map; it would not be long before they docked at Agia Roumeli. Georgia took a deep breath and descended from the top deck to find the guide and the rest of the group. Her companions were English and after she had greeted them they were surprised to hear her speaking Greek to the guide. Hesitatingly she was drawn into conversation, her companions eager to know how someone they had all assumed was English spoke such fluent Greek.

Put on the spot, not wanting to be rude, she explained that although she was born in England her father was Greek and had always encouraged her to speak the language. Surprisingly, Georgia found herself relaxing into the company, something she had recently found difficult with strangers. Until then she had been reticent about going on the trek, but now she found that she was excited at the prospect of hiking the gorge.

Passengers stood and moved towards the bow, eager to disembark. Agia Roumeli was small, accessible only by boat or on foot through the gorge. The village was quiet, in hushed anticipation of the many hikers who would arrive in a few hours' time having trekked down the gorge from Xyloskalo. Few, it appeared, were taking the route from here as the guide led her charges along a path crossing a bed of rocks. Although it was early in the morning, the sun reflected off the sea and the boulders strewn on the beach. Georgia reached in her bag for a bottle of water. An elderly goatherd stood watching them, his chin resting on his crook, his herd tinkling their way across the stony lowland between the sea and the entrance to the gorge. He called to his dog, and nodded in response to Georgia's greeting of *kalimera*, his face inscrutable.

As they entered the canyon, Georgia was grateful for the shade of the mountains rising up on either side. The path followed the course of a burbling stream and Georgia wondered how this benign trickle could in any way have contributed to the creation of the spectacular landscape. The guide stopped and explained that throughout winter, the stream was swollen with rainfall and melt-water from the snows on the mountain peaks. During these months the Samaria Park was closed as the torrent of water made walking there too dangerous.

The path began to climb more steeply and Georgia had to concentrate to keep her footing on the rocks. They crossed the stream on wooden bridges as the sides of the gorge closed in on them. High above, trees clung precariously to the rock face and with every step Georgia had to crane her neck further to see the sky.

The guide stopped at a spot where the canyon squeezed in on them so much that Georgia felt as though she could almost touch both sides. She stretched out her arms, but fell short by several feet. These were the famed *sideroportes* or iron gates, the narrowest section. Looking upwards, the rock faces towered for what Georgia thought must be at least 1,000 feet, and she stood in awe, breathing in the majesty.

'Let's move down the track for a moment,' said the guide, ushering the group back the way they had come to where the path widened. A donkey was being led across the uneven rocks towards them.

'An ambulance,' the guide explained. 'If someone hurts themselves on the trail, it's the only way to get them out.'

As Georgia squeezed her back against the cold rock face, she saw the injured man looking at her. He was obviously in pain and catching her momentary glance he looked shocked and she dropped her gaze, embarrassed to be intruding on this difficult moment.

Resuming their hike, the guide led them back through the *sideroportes*. 'I'll wait here for you for fifteen minutes so you can explore and take photographs, then we'll return to Agia Roumeli for lunch and a swim before catching the ferry back to Paleochora.'

The gorge was already starting to get busy with hikers who had made an early start from the top when it opened at seven o'clock. As Georgia walked further up the path she had to keep stopping to let others pass. She turned and walked back to join the guide sitting on a rock beside the stream.

She dabbled her feet in the icy water as it gurgled its way towards the sea. Refreshed, she let the sun dry her and as the rest of the group joined them Georgia pulled on her socks and boots and followed as they made their way back down.

Over lunch, Georgia made small talk. She gave nothing of herself away but was happy that she did not feel the crippling self-consciousness she often suffered in the company of strangers. They lingered long over their desserts, finishing off the wine and raki. Georgia wondered about the wisdom of having a swim but, when they reached the beach, she was grateful to immerse herself in the cooling balm of the sea. Her legs had begun to ache and as she floated looking up at the sky, her mind wandered to the injured man on the donkey. Should she have offered to help? He would have to wait for a boat out of the village, either to Chora Sfakion or maybe he would be on the ferry back to Paleochora?

*

Jack had left Epano Elounda and driven to Chania the previous day, staying overnight in a hotel near the outskirts of the city. He had ordered a taxi to pick him up in time to get him to the head of the gorge as soon as it opened, keen to make an early start. The driver swung the black Mercedes around the hairpin bends and as dawn broke he could make out the sheer drops just inches from the wheels as they threaded their way into the White Mountains.

Jack felt excited by the prospect of the challenge. He smiled as the driver took a hand off the steering wheel to cross himself as they passed a roadside shrine on a precarious bend. They arrived early in Xyloskalo, the starting point of the trek, and the sun began to fill in the colours of the trees and rocks as it rose, a breathtaking accompaniment to the inviting silence which whetted Jack's appetite for the walk ahead.

Jack paid his entrance fee, impatient to get started. He set off on a path which quickly turned into a steep drop down steps into a valley densely forested with cypresses and pines. He breathed in the smells of pine and eucalyptus and felt his spirit lift at the seclusion.

It had been his decision to return to Crete to see if he could rebuild his life after the trauma that had almost taken it from him. His idea was to write a book as he took on the physical challenges of walking the coastal paths, climbing the mountains and hiking the dramatic gorges of the island. He hoped that in testing his body he could improve his wellbeing and perhaps find a way to make a living. The counsellor, who had been paid for by the charitable fund which his father had encouraged him to approach, agreed to the plan Jack had proposed. Within weeks of the idea having formed in his head, Jack had been on a plane for Crete.

He relished the prospect of the walk which would see him descend 4,000 feet from high up on the Omalos Plateau and walk some ten miles to the village of Agia Roumeli on the coast. From there he would catch a ferry to Chora Sfakion, where that evening he would get a taxi to return him to Chania.

His new leg was comfortable, and he made good progress. In little more than a couple of hours he came across the lonely chapel of Agios Nikolaos standing beside the trickling river. Keen to stay ahead of the walkers who would be following him down the trail, he set off towards the abandoned village of Samaria, after which the gorge took its name. Here he stopped to take a drink and eat a banana. Sitting down, he noticed his back was beginning to stiffen, but he was enjoying the walk. He looked around but could not see any of the cautious kri-kri, the Cretan ibex, an endangered species and one of the reasons the

Samaria National Park was established as a nature reserve. It was the middle of the morning and checking with his map he thought he was about halfway. Swinging his bag onto his shoulders he strode out downhill into the narrowing canyon. High above, something cast a shadow over the shaft of light which slithered between the vertical faces of the rock. He looked upwards and caught sight of a golden eagle gliding effortlessly on a thermal.

Distracted, he missed his footing and fell; he heard a bone crack before he felt the searing pain in his ankle. For how long he was unconscious he did not know, but when he came round there was a man kneeling beside him urging him to take a drink of water. Standing behind his rescuer Jack could make out a donkey. The man explained that he was a park ranger and that the only way they could get Jack out was using the donkey ambulance. He would give him some pain relief and strap his ankle. The donkey would transport him to Agia Roumeli from where he would be taken to Chora Sfakion by ferry, then an ambulance would transport him to hospital in Chania.

Another two rangers appeared. Jack was dozy with pain relief and the heat but somehow they manoeuvred him into the saddle, securing him as best they could with straps, and set off down the uneven track through the gorge, one leading the donkey and the other holding him stable. He felt himself drifting in and out of consciousness. The sunlight dimmed and he couldn't distinguish whether it was the mountains drawing in on him or the effect of the analgesics. He blinked and tried to keep his eyes open. He was relieved to see the two sheer faces of the gorge narrowing and knew he was not hallucinating. In front of him some hikers were gathering at the point where the vertical cliffs were closest together. The group turned round and descended to where the path was wide enough for them to pass.

He tried to say thank you but was unsure if any words came out. A woman with long dark hair, sparkling brown eyes and a slender fragile beauty caught his eye. It took just seconds for him to realise that he had seen her before and seconds more for him to remember where, but by then she had looked away and in that moment she was gone as the donkey was led further down the gorge. His mind wandered to his graduation day in Exeter and the young doctor he had met. He was sure the woman was Georgia. Why had she not said anything? He was certain that she had seen him. As they progressed onto the track which took them the last mile and a half to Agia Roumeli, he found himself descending into a dark place. She had ignored him.

He struggled to think what his therapist would have said, no doubt that Georgia had not recognised him – after all, his hair was now much shorter and he had grown a beard. He knew that when he was at a low ebb he was self-conscious about his injury. He asked himself why he should care so much about what she thought of him, a woman he hardly knew, but was rescued from these thoughts as the painkillers began to wear off and the discomfort in his ankle progressed from a dull ache to agony.

In Agia Roumeli he was made comfortable until a ferry arrived, and then was transferred to the boat for the journey to Chora Sfakion where an ambulance awaited his arrival. The paramedics put in an intravenous drip to administer more pain relief for his journey across the White Mountains to hospital in Chania.

The operation to realign and fix his broken ankle was routine and done that same night. By the next day, Jack was sitting up in bed and eating. He was keen to get out of the hospital but could not drive or walk on crutches and even if he could get a suitable wheelchair, he would not be able to get it up the steps to the front door of the house in Elounda.

He had been trying to avoid phoning his parents with the news of his accident. They had done so much for him already and it seemed as though he was always relying on them to get him out of his difficulties. He was, after all, a grown man. In a couple of years he would be thirty. What had he got to show for it, at a time when many people had partners, even families and a home of their own and a steady job? He had his work as a writer, but every time he was making progress with that, life would deal him a blow that set him back.

A picture of the woman he had passed in the gorge was lodged in his head. He had been sure it was Georgia, the girl he had met back in Exeter on the night of his graduation. He felt a glimmer of comfort at the thought of her face, then recalled how she had ignored him. Why would she want anything to do with him, a disabled man with nothing to offer? Reaching out to the bedside cabinet he picked up his phone and dialled his mother's number.

'What were you thinking of attempting to walk the gorge on your own?' Ginny admonished her son after she had recovered from the shock of learning he was in hospital. 'I'll speak to your father and one or both of us will be with you as soon as we can. We'll call you back when we've managed to find a flight.'

Knowing that someone would be flying out to help filled him with reassurance but he was also frustrated that he had not been able to cope on his own. He knew he had to accept support or languish in hospital until his ankle had recovered.

His parents managed to book a flight to Chania that evening and hoped to arrive at the hospital in the early hours of the following day. He looked forward to seeing them, and the wait until they arrived seemed interminable. Every few hours a nurse would come to his bedside to check the monitors and take his temperature and blood pressure. In between these visits he would doze, or lie awake mulling over in his head how life had brought him there.

In the silence of the sleeping hospital, he awoke to the sound of his parents speaking quietly to a nurse who ushered them onto the ward. His mother bent to kiss him and he could see a tear in her eye. His father patted him on a shoulder. They were exhausted and after Jack had told the story of his accident, they fell asleep in the chairs at his bedside.

The morning routine of the hospital woke them and while Ginny went to find breakfast, Stephen set about making arrangements to get his son back to Epano Elounda. He had already hired a car from the airport and arranged to have Jack's rental vehicle picked up from the hotel where he had left it. He then enquired of the hospital staff where he could hire a wheelchair and was directed to a nearby medical centre which rented out mobility aids. When the doctors were satisfied their patient would have suitable care, they discharged him on the proviso he contact the hospital in Agios Nikolaos to provide backup care and physiotherapy.

Jack felt immense relief as he was wheeled by his father out of the hospital to the car.

*

After three days convalescing, Jack had an appointment at the hospital in Agios Nikolaos. The doctor was adamant it would be a minimum of six weeks before he could put weight on the ankle.

'And when will he be fit to fly? His father asked.

'He can fly now,' replied the doctor. 'But he will need the cast split for the journey and another X-ray and a new cast put on when he reaches his destination.'

'That's OK; I won't be needing to do that as I'm staying on here.' Jack looked at his father whose face gave away his surprise but said nothing.

'In that case I will organise for a physiotherapist who will come to your house in the village to give you exercises,' the doctor said, and made a note on Jack's record. 'As you are young and fit he will try to get you walking on crutches, with luck it will get you a bit more mobile. I will also arrange for you to have another X-ray in a few weeks to see how things are healing.'

As Stephen pulled out of the hospital car park, Jack knew he had to say something to his father.

'I'm sorry Dad, I should have said earlier. I've decided to keep to my original plans.' He looked across at his father who nodded.

'Of course, if that's what you want. But I will need to get back home to work in the next two weeks, are you sure you'll be able to cope on your own?'

'That's just my point, Dad. You and Mum are always dropping everything to look after me. It's not that I'm not grateful, I am. I know I phoned and asked for your help, but, if you'll excuse the pun, I need to learn to stand on my own two feet. I cannot keep going backwards in life. I want to stay here and continue trying to write my book. At least not being mobile might help me concentrate on getting more work done.'

Within a week, on his crutches Jack was able to navigate the two steps into the house and walk the short distance along the lane to the village taverna.

'You see, now I have everything I need,' Jack laughed as Alexander welcomed them with raki.

'This will make you better,' Alexander raised a glass. 'I heard about your accident and that you prefer to travel by donkey these days.'

Jack looked surprised.

'You are in Crete. News travels fast. And so do you – you are walking already!'

When Ginny and Stephen explained that they would be leaving in a week's time, Alexander could sense their concern for their son. Standing, he hugged Ginny.

'Don't worry; the village will look after him.'

Chapter 8

2024

IT WAS HARD to escape the unforgiving heat as summer blazed in. He did his best to rise early and take a walk before the sun was too high in the sky, returning for breakfast after which he would sit at his table and try to write. He would take another walk during the early evening before visiting the local taverna for dinner.

Alexander was as good as his word and would take him into Elounda when he visited to order food for his business. At first Jack struggled, his arms and back ached from walking even the shortest distance. But his determination paid off, and his muscles regained the strength they had developed after losing his leg.

With the strain of exercising in the heat, he was losing weight which in turn made it easier to get about on his crutches.

After three weeks he arranged for a taxi to take him to Agios Nikolaos for a doctor's appointment at the hospital. The consultant was happy with the progress he had made. The swelling on the ankle had reduced considerably and the doctor cut off the plaster and instructed a technician to apply a new one, which he hoped could be removed on Jack's next visit in another three weeks.

If Jack was making good progress in getting himself back to full fitness, his writing was not coming along so well. It had been his intention to write a narrative about his personal experiences of Crete, but not being able to get around the island, he felt limited in what he could write about. He would start the day with good intentions, but all too often his mind would drift from his work. He would get disheartened by the few words he had managed to piece together and snap the lid of the laptop down in frustration, giving up for another day. He was grateful to Alexander for taking him to Elounda some mornings, but the taverna owner had a business to run, so Jack never got to spend more than an hour or two in the town.

He reminded himself that the doctor had said it might only be a few weeks before the plaster came off and he could begin to use his leg. He hoped then that he could hire an automatic car and continue his exploration of the island.

As he got stronger his walks around the village became more ambitious and he began to meet more people, smile and reply to their greetings. As they became more familiar, some were keen to ask about his injuries and what he was doing in the village. He made friends with a group of ex-pats who would sometimes meet in the taverna, some of whom lived in the village and others further away. He was grateful for their company as he often felt loneliness stalking him.

The day before his next hospital appointment began to drag and Jack was impatient. He could not concentrate on his work at all but was too listless to read and it was too hot during the day for him to snooze the time away. He arrived at the taverna earlier than usual. The heat was still stifling and it was a bit early for him to eat. He took a seat in the shade at one of the tables Alexander had set out on the road. He ordered a cold beer, and with his taverna empty, Alexander sat with him until the first customers began to arrive.

'It's Jack isn't it?' Jack looked up to see a woman and a man approaching. 'I never got to thank you for mentioning us in the newspaper article you wrote a few years ago. We own the boat that does the marine safari tours.'

'Popi, Costa?' From somewhere, despite only having met them briefly three years ago, Jack managed to conjure the couple's names. 'Of course I remember.'

'We heard you were here, and about your accidents. I'm so sorry.' Popi looked down, embarrassed.

'Don't be,' Jack said, eager to put the young woman at ease. 'With a bit of luck I'll get the plaster off tomorrow. And the other leg, well that's old news. Would you like a drink, we could move inside and find a bigger table if you'd like to join me.'

'If you don't mind?' said Costas. 'We haven't a tour this evening so we thought we'd come out for dinner.'

'I'd be pleased of the company. I get a bit of cabin fever stuck up here much of the time. Can't wait to get this off,' Jack held up his plastered leg, 'and be able to get about a bit more.'

Going inside, Alexander pointed them to a table beneath an open window before coming over to take their drink order and leaving the tick box menus. 'I also have moussaka this evening, as well as all the usual mezzes.'

Alexander brought the carafe of white wine they had ordered along with bread, olives and a beetroot, lemon and oil dip and they all decided to have moussaka and share a large salad. As they drank, Jack found himself opening up to the friendly couple. So much had happened since their previous meeting and he found himself explaining how he had lost his leg chasing stories in Ukraine and, after deciding to return to Crete to recuperate, had injured himself hiking the Samaria Gorge.

'I remember you asking us about dolphins when we met. Well, since then they appear to be coming closer inshore, although I have not yet seen one in the bay,' said Popi. 'I did hear a fisherman the other day say he had spotted one down near Plaka, although he might have imagined it,' she laughed. 'But I've read that they are coming closer inshore to find food as the oceans warm up and the fish stocks dwindle, and we do see them more often now out at sea.'

'You should come out with us on the boat one day,' Costas added. 'See how you feel when the plaster comes off tomorrow. We could go around to the bays on the other side of Kalidon and maybe to Olous, a swim might help you get some strength back in your ankle. I'll give you our number and when you feel up to it we can organise a trip. Our way of saying thank you for the publicity your article gave us.'

The following day, Jack felt a sense of liberation when the doctor cut the plaster from his ankle. It felt strange putting weight on that leg again, and he was advised to build up using it gradually, continuing on the crutches to aid his rehabilitation.

Jack was determined but sensible, and he was soon managing to get up the stairs to the terrace. Being able to sit outside and drink his early-morning coffee or in the evening watch the sunset over the bay lifted his spirits and his mind began to turn to his writing. He was keen to expand his horizons further than the village.

Several days after he had first managed to climb the stairs he was sitting in the morning sunshine staring down on the bay. It was still early and the water looked like glass. On the other side of the causeway, off the smart hotels to the east, a large yacht lay at anchor. From the quay in Elounda below he could see the first ferry of the day setting course for Spinalonga. Around the headland of Kalidon a caique ploughed a white furrow across the Bay of Mirabello before slowing and coming to rest, dropping anchor near the canal. He was certain he recognised it as Popi and Costas' boat and remembered their offer. How he would love to be on the bay and maybe Costas was right, a swim might help strengthen his ankle. He had not been swimming since losing his leg. Perhaps with his new friends' help he could get back in the water.

*

Costas offered a hand to Jack as he stepped onto the short gangplank which bridged the quay and the cockpit of the boat.

He was impressed to see the progress that Jack had already made as he insisted getting onto the caique himself.

'I'm really looking forward to today,' said Jack. 'It's so kind of you to take me out.'

'It's a pleasure. It's nice to get out without having to attend to paying guests.' Popi raised the gangplank and let go the stern line as Costas directed the boat into the bay and turned the tiller, steering for Spinalonga. Jack could make out the village of Epano Elounda amongst the olive groves which shrouded the mountainside. An occasional spray tickled his face and the breeze as the caique made way towards the island was welcome as the sun rose in the sky. As they got closer he saw tourists, like a swarm of ants, disembarking onto the island from a large boat. He remembered the time he had first visited the old leper colony with his parents as a child.

Costas expertly navigated among the anchored ferries and pleasure craft into the narrow channel between Kalidon and Spinalonga, and Jack felt the slight pitch of the vessel as the sheltered waters met the open sea. He looked up at the imposing walls of the Venetian fort which had for centuries guarded the bay from the attentions of invading forces and pirates. The boat turned broadside on to the slight swell, taking on a comfortable roll as they hugged the deserted cliffs of Kalidon.

From the cabin below, Popi brought up fresh orange juice and spinach pies. While they sat eating and drinking, she pointed out goats grazing on the hillsides and a row of cormorants perched on a rock. Costas steered into shore, bringing the bow of the caique close enough for Popi to jump off and scoop sea salt from a rock pool, bringing it back aboard for Jack to sample. They steered into a secluded bay, a tiny chapel near the waterfront.

At the eastern headland of Kalidon they passed a tourist boat, its passengers drinking and dancing to music blaring from speakers. They felt the craft's wake slap against the caique as the noise of its passing faded into the distance. Costas turned the boat into the Bay of Mirabello and Jack could make out the chapel of Analipsi and the canal beyond. An elderly man was fishing as he sat on the rocks in the shadow of a tree, a bucket by his feet. Jack could now see they had sailed all the way around the island of Kalidon, and Costas explained that the canal was too narrow and the bridge too low for a boat like *Katerina* to pass through.

Near the entrance to the canal, Costas released the windlass. The anchor dropped to the sea bed before the engine was cut and there was blissful silence. The causeway looked as though it was hovering on the shimmering sea. On the other side he could see the Bay of Korfos where people were swimming off the beach, mountains encircling the bay, and in the distance high above the island of Spinalonga he saw the wind turbines. He recalled his walk to the deserted lighthouse when he had seen the dolphins. That was the day he had first met Popi and Costas. It seemed like an eternity ago. So much had happened to him and the world during that time. He had just been setting out to become a freelance writer, a journey which had eventually taken him to a war zone and the loss of his leg. Now he had come full circle and was again trying to find a way in the world.

His eyes followed a small boat as it made its way under the low stone bridge which joined Kalidon to the causeway. From the shore he heard the screams of two children as their father stood in the water splashing them, encouraging them to take the plunge and swim out over the lost city. He remembered the time he had first visited Crete and had swum here. He was rescued from his thoughts by a splash, and then Popi surfaced in the water. 'Are you coming in? It's lovely and warm.'

Before the trip he had embraced the challenge of going in the water but now the thought filled him with fear. The boat was anchored in deep water, what he thought to be at least five metres.

'Here, these will support you,' said Costas, reaching down and pulling two bright red swimming noodles from a locker. 'There is a platform at the back of the boat. Popi and I can help you.'

'I've got my swimming shorts on. I might as well give it a try.' Jack heard himself say, his words belying his anxiety.

Jack took off his prosthetic leg and sat on the edge of the cockpit. He swung himself round and down onto the platform. Costas threw the noodles to Popi in the water and supported Jack as he lowered himself down the two steps of the ladder into the water. Popi put a float under each arm as he let go and Costas followed him into the warm sea.

Jack turned on his back, buoyed by the salty water. He edged the noodles from under his arms and let go. He was floating. Elated he lay there, trying to get a sense of his body in the water. He rolled onto his front and stretched out his arms, pulling against the water in a crawl stroke. It took him some time to adjust to the feeling of swimming again, but twisting his head to breathe, he could see Costas alongside him which gave him confidence.

He turned onto his back again, revelling in the liberation of being in the water and proud of his achievement. It had been some time since he had felt such joy and he felt a smile break across his face. He looked up at the sky before closing his eyes and letting himself float, weightless, he did not know for how long. When at last he looked around, he saw the reassuring presence of Costas treading water nearby, the anchored caique about four metres away, and began to swim towards it. Aboard the boat he could see Popi taking pictures.

'You'll have to send them to me,' Jack shouted as he grabbed for the steps.

'I'll go first.' Costas put his foot on the boarding ladder and climbed onto the platform. If getting into the water had been daunting, getting out took all Jack's strength. His arms were tired and reluctantly he allowed Costas to reach down and help him up.

Delving into his pack he got out his towel and carefully dried himself before refitting his leg and pulling on a T-shirt.

'Would you like a drink?' Without waiting for an answer, Popi handed the two men a beer from the cool-box, taking one herself before sitting down in the cockpit.

'Thank you, for the beer and taking me swimming. It was incredible. What a great day.' It had been some time since Jack had felt so elated.

'And it's not over yet,' replied Costas. 'We haven't had the lunch Popi's made us. You're probably hungry after that.'

Popi began to bring up the food she had prepared at home earlier that morning and put it on the table. They tucked in to roast chicken and potatoes, salad, fava and tzatziki along with a metal jug of wine.

Over lunch they talked about how Jack was trying to write a book about Crete but how his plans had stalled after his fall in the Samaria Gorge. Following the swim he had found a renewed optimism for his project and was excited as his new friends gave him suggestions of walks and places he might like to include. Sitting with Popi and Costas, he realised how he enjoyed being in their company and how recently he had been isolated, particularly since his hiking accident.

'We have to get back,' Popi said looking at her watch. 'I've got a group coming for a Stars and Legends cruise this evening and we need to get the food and drink ready for that.'

Costas helped his wife clear the table before she started the engine and Jack heard the anchor chain being raised. Popi pushed the tiller, steering the vessel close inshore to Kalidon. A welcome breeze had got up and a slight spray cooled Jack's face as the caique comfortably slid over the oncoming swell. Costas went below, returning with the carafe refilled, and topped up their glasses as they sat talking over the throbbing engine.

As Popi navigated the rocks in the narrow entrance to the Bay of Korfos, the walls on the fortress of Spinalonga were busy with tourists. Some of the more energetic visitors had made their way to the hill which topped the island and stood waving. The channel was crowded with boats dropping and picking up their cargo of passengers or waiting at anchor in the bay. Leaving the island behind, Popi steered the vessel towards Elounda and its mooring on the quayside at the taverna.

The gangplank lowered, Costas offered Jack his hand. He politely refused, determined to make his own way onto dry land.

'Thank you for today,' Jack said as Popi hugged him.

'We must do it again sometime,' said Costas. 'Now that summer is coming to an end we will have more time and the water stays warm for swimming well into autumn.' Jack grinned at the invitation.

'You've got our number if you need anything,' said Popi, 'and we're in The Boatyard most nights after the evening cruise if you fancy a drink and some company.' Jack felt warm inside as he could tell that her invitation was heartfelt. 'I'll take you up on that. I can't thank you enough, especially for helping me to swim again.'

'We've enjoyed it too,' replied Costas. 'We'll see you soon I hope.'

Although Jack was tired he walked to the square to find a taxi to take him home. He had a renewed sense that things were possible. Back at the village house he climbed the stairs with a new vigour and opened the door onto the terrace, letting the early-evening light spread over the room. He returned downstairs and poured himself a glass of wine before climbing back up. Under the pergola in the shade of the deep red bougainvillea he looked at the lemon and olive trees his mother had potted when they had first bought the house. He walked to the wall which surrounded the balcony and gazed down on the bay. He spotted Popi and Costas' caique making its way out to sea as the light began to fade. He lit the candle lanterns and lifted them onto the wall before going inside and making the bed in the upstairs bedroom. From now on he would sleep in there. Climbing the stairs would do him good.

He sat down, and stared over the pantiled rooftops and the olive groves. Somewhere on the mountainside above he heard the bleating of goats and closer the creak of the metal bird which topped the chimney as it turned on the breeze. The lights were going on in Elounda and a sprinkling of stars began to dot the sky. Jack heard his phone ping. He smiled as he opened the message from Popi and photos of him swimming appeared on his screen. He had not looked at the pictures on his phone for some time and as he scrolled through his photos he came to a selfie he had taken at the top of the Samaria Gorge holding onto a wooden rail, the tree-lined mountains dropping away behind him. Another picture came into his mind, the face of Georgia turning away from him as he was taken out of the canyon by donkey. Why would she have recognised him? His hair had been cut short, unlike the long, flowing locks he had worn as a student, he was older, his complexion tanned and his unshaven face drawn with pain. Perhaps he had been wrong in thinking she did not want to engage with him. He let his thoughts go back to the night of their graduation and how they had walked beside the estuary in Topsham.

Looking through his pictures he eventually found the shot he had taken five years ago, the river behind them as yachts with their sails unfurled headed seawards. How happy he had looked that morning standing with a beautiful girl he had just met. He remembered her saying that her father was from Crete and that her grandmother still lived here. He tried to remember where she had said they visited. He went inside and got a map. It was in the south-west of the island, he recalled. He drew his finger along the coast. Paleochora, that jolted his memory. Yes, he was sure that's what Georgia had said. Searching on his phone he found her number in his contacts and, taking a deep breath, dialled.

The number was not found. He felt his mood plummet. She had probably returned home by now, anyway.

Over the coming days he could not let the thought of trying to find Georgia rest. He knew it was probably destined to failure, but told himself that a journey to the south-west of the island would in any case give him useful material for his book, which he had decided would be a collection of short anecdotal pieces, his own impressions of the island.

He visited The Boatyard one evening to meet up with Popi and Costas, and explained what he intended to his friends.

'I think that's very romantic,' said Popi encouragingly when he showed her Georgia's picture on his phone.

'This is Crete, and Paleochora is not a big place. Most people know the other families in the village. I'm sure someone will recognise her,' Costas reassured him. 'Especially as she is so beautiful.' Popi jokingly punched her husband on the arm.

Jack's ankle was much stronger and he decided if he could hire an automatic car he would be able to drive. Days later he was behind the wheel. The driving was the easy bit. Now he was set on going to Paleochora, he was nervous. What would he say if he found Georgia?

Initially he planned to make overnight stops in Rethymnon and Chania and do some research for his book but as he drove further west along the main highway he felt his anxiety begin to kick in and knew that if he delayed he might lose his nerve. It was afternoon by the time he turned off the main road and headed south. As he drove he recalled that the last time he had been near here, in a taxi heading for the Samaria Gorge, was the same day he had seen Georgia less than three months before. Again, doubt began to worm its way into his head. What if he did find her and she didn't remember him, or worse, didn't want to see him? Anyway, he suspected she had gone home already, back to her job as a doctor. The road zigzagged its way down the mountains to the Libyan Sea. Approaching Paleochora, it flattened onto the peninsula which led to the town and Jack felt the tension rise inside him.

He was hungry and tired from the journey and thought it best to find accommodation for the night. He followed the road which skirted the town, arriving to the west of the harbour. Here he decided to park and walk back into the warren of narrow streets. He did not have to go far. Across the road from a large sandy beach he found a taverna advertising rooms to rent. He was in luck, the owner showed him to a basic apartment and within minutes of arriving he was in the restaurant looking at the menu. It was late afternoon and he was the only customer. The man who had shown him the room came to his table to take his drinks order, taking the time to chat, asking where Jack had come from.

'Elounda, it is lovely there, but a long way to drive in a day?' The owner raised his eyes.

'I'm writing a book, and thought Paleochora would be a good base from which to explore the southwest of the island,' Jack answered.

'Oh it is, from here you can go by boat to Elafonisi or walk the gorges of Samaria or Imbros, or take a ferry to Loutro or even Chora Sfakion. You will find plenty to write about.'

'Also,' Jack hesitated before reaching in his pocket and pulling out his phone. 'I am looking for an old friend.' He clicked on the photo and held it up for the owner to see.

'I know her. Well, I don't know her, but I know who she is. She is Maria's granddaughter from England. She was staying with Maria this summer but I don't know if she is still here.'

Jack could not believe his luck that he might have found her. 'Do you have a number I could have?' he asked excitedly.

'No, I don't have. She lives only two kilometres along this road in a house beside the sea. It's easy to find. The drive goes onto the beach and is opposite a large yellow villa. It is very near.'

Jack thought it would be rude to leave immediately. He ordered pork chops and a glass of wine. Whilst waiting for the food to arrive his mind churned with what he would say to Georgia when he met her, if she had not already left the island. When it came he had lost his appetite but he ate as much of his meal as he could so as not to offend the owner and drank the wine to give himself courage.

The pebbles scrunched under the tyres as he turned into a driveway which ran across the beach. The house was surrounded by a well-tended garden of succulents growing through the stones and geraniums in terracotta pots shaded by tamarisk trees.

He brought the vehicle to a halt next to a white car. Getting out, he could hear the sound of whispering waves. Looking behind the house he could see the beach, deserted. The stones sounded loud under his feet as he made his way to the door and knocked. He waited nervously for what was less than a minute, but seemed like an eternity. He was about to knock again when he heard footsteps inside and the door opened.

'I'm sorry. We were sitting on the terrace out the back.' The young woman stopped and stared, a glimmer of recognition in her eyes.

'Do you remember me? Jack, from university.' He extended his hand.

Georgia's face broke into a wide smile as he stepped forward.

Chapter 9

2024

'JACK. OF COURSE. But what are you doing here?'

Faced with the question from Georgia, although he had been going over answers in his head for ages, he could not come up with one.

'Why don't you come in and meet my *yiayia*.' Georgia broke the silence, ushering him through the house to the terrace.

'Granny, this is Jack.' She introduced him to the bright-eyed elderly lady sitting in the shade of a yellow-striped sun canopy. 'He's a friend of mine.'

Jack felt himself warm at those words.

'I thought I saw you some weeks ago in the Samaria Gorge,' Jack said by way of explanation at his being there. 'But I was a bit indisposed and couldn't stop.'

Georgia looked at him quizzically.

'I'd broken my ankle, and was on a donkey. I was a bit spaced out at the time,' he said, sheepishly.

'Was that you who passed us near the *sideroportes*? I saw the donkey ambulance, but didn't like to stare. But you're OK now?'

So she hadn't recognised him. Jack felt relief. 'Yes, getting there. I tried to phone later but couldn't get through.'

'I've changed my number, I was getting too many nuisance calls.'

'Why don't you sit down, Jack?' Georgia's grandmother indicated a chair. 'I'm Maria. I think it's that time of day when we could have a glass of wine. Georgia, would you mind?'

Jack followed the young woman with his eyes as she disappeared into the house. He saw Maria watching him, the hint of a smile on her face as she sat taking in the early evening sun. Georgia returned with a tray on which were three glasses and a jug of wine. Jack stood to take the tray from her but she motioned him to sit down. Close up she was even more beautiful than he remembered. He looked away as she put the tray on the table.

'Is your ankle still giving you problems?' Georgia asked, noticing a slight limp as Jack sat back down.

'Of course, you're a doctor.' Jack saw the young woman look down as he spoke. 'Actually the limp is in my other leg, the ankle is fine now.' He self-consciously lifted his trouser leg to reveal the bottom of his prosthetic. 'I did a bit more lasting damage to this one.'

'Oh, I'm sorry. I didn't know. Not much of a doctor, am I?' Georgia paused. 'In fact, I'm not sure I'm a doctor at all.'

Jack noticed Maria push herself to her feet. 'I'll go inside and get us some snacks to have with our drinks,' she said as she walked through the patio doors into the house.

Turning his gaze on Georgia, he could see she was trembling slightly and beads of sweat had broken out on her forehead. 'You first,' she said quietly, holding his gaze.

'Are you alright?' Jack asked, concerned.

'Don't worry. I get like this sometimes. Tell me what happened to your leg.'

As Jack embarked on the story, Maria returned, putting a bowl of olives and some mixed nuts on the table. 'I'm feeling a little bit tired. So if you don't mind I think I'll go and have a late nap. You two clearly have some catching up to do.'

Georgia raised her eyes and smiled as her grandmother disappeared back inside.

With Georgia's encouragement Jack resumed. There was little he held back on, opening up about his struggles working at the newspaper before finding his way as a freelance journalist in control of his own work, although he had to admit that the support of his parents allowed him the financial security to pursue that path. He told of his thrill at working in a war zone in Ukraine, and how he was lucky to be alive after being traumatically wounded in a drone attack. He explained how he had come to Crete to aid his rehabilitation and try and resurrect his career.

'That is how I came to be in the Samaria Gorge, when I stupidly tripped and broke my ankle and found myself on the back of a donkey. I was sure it was you I saw that day, but didn't know how I'd find you until I discovered the picture we took that morning in Topsham. And here I am. There we go; a potted history of five years of misadventure. Now, how about you?'

At first Georgia found it hard to open up about the intervening years since they had last met. Jack felt empathy with her struggles and was a good listener. She surprised herself by opening up about her whirlwind romance with Rory and his tragic death and her subsequent struggles working throughout the pandemic years and her eventual breakdown. She admitted she had given up working as a doctor and was here in Crete to try and recuperate. Jack gave her a shoulder to cry on, absorbing the pain of her grief along with her tears, and though embarrassed by revealing her emotions to a man she hardly knew, in telling him she felt strangely better.

Maria's snooze was longer than she might usually have had, and when she emerged she found her granddaughter deep in conversation with the handsome young man who had appeared out of the blue. To the west the sun was blazing orange as it approached the watery horizon.

'What a beautiful sunset,' Jack said, looking at Maria. 'What a fantastic spot to have a house.'

'I'm very lucky, from here I can watch the sun rise every morning and the sun go down each evening,' Maria replied.

'Jack's writing a book about Crete,' Georgia explained.

'So you came to Paleochora to do some research?' Maria raised an eye.

'Well, not exactly,' Jack admitted. 'But while I'm here it would be a shame not to take advantage of the trip. Where do you think I should visit?'

'Well you probably won't want to do the gorge,' Georgia said, laughing. But there's Elafonisi, Sougia, Chora Sfakion. Have you been to Loutro? We could go on the ferry, tomorrow.' Georgia stopped. 'I'm sorry, I didn't mean to…'

'Yes,' interrupted Jack. 'I'd like that.'

When Jack returned to the pension he was tired, but found it hard to sleep. Things could not have gone better. He had found Georgia more easily than he could have hoped and not only was he reassured that she had not blanked him that day in the gorge, but they were going on a date the following day. Sometime in the early hours he must have dropped off but he woke early, full of anticipation for the trip to Loutro.

He walked to the town quay, stopping at the ticket agency on the way and still had time to go to a nearby bakery to buy croissants. He resisted the temptation to eat his breakfast there and then but decided to wait for Georgia and sat on one of the yellow-topped bollards. He felt his heart lift as he saw her walking towards him.

'I got our tickets so we've no need to rush. And here's some breakfast,' Jack said, handing her a bag. 'I didn't know if you'd have time to eat.'

'I had a yoghurt. My grandmother won't let me out of the house if I haven't had something, but I can always eat a croissant, thank you.' She took the bag and put it in her backpack. 'I'll have it when we get on board.'

A short line of cars had formed on the quay by the time the ferry had docked and dropped its ramp. Georgia and Jack joined the other foot passengers boarding and climbed to the top deck to claim seats from where they would get a good view of the coastline. As they sat, Georgia was reminded of the last time she had taken this journey. The same day that Jack had broken his ankle, an event which led to him coming to Paleochora to find her. Jack delved into his paper bag. 'I'm going to eat, I'm starving.' Following suit, Georgia took her croissant from her pack and bit into it. She brushed the flakes of pastry from her lips and Jack watched as they floated down towards the waters below. A lock of hair broke free from the bunch behind her head. Absent-mindedly she drew it back behind an ear.

Jack snapped a picture, looking at it before handing his phone to Georgia for her approval. 'That's a lovely shot of you.'

'I hate pictures of myself,' Georgia replied, staring out at the mountains ashore. For a moment she recognised the familiar dark shadow which passed over the happiness she had been feeling. She shook her head slightly to dislodge the thoughts that threatened to drag her down. She tried to focus on the morning sun reflecting off the mirrored sea. How, amidst all this beauty, could she still succumb to the guilt and fear which over the last years she had carried with her?

A RIB sped past, the group of divers aboard laughing and waving. Georgia watched as Jack waved back, and raised an arm. As the dive boat barrelled its way towards the shore, the ferry followed in its wake towards Sougia. From above, the pair watched as they moored on the quay for just long enough to let off three cars and take aboard a handful of walkers before the lines were cast off and the ship set out again.

Georgia stood at the rail. The wind ruffled her hair and she lifted a hand to stop it blowing in her eyes as she looked towards the strip of buildings dwarfed by the towering mountains.

'There's Agia Roumeli. I can't see the entrance to the gorge from here.'

'I don't remember it from my last visit,' replied Jack. 'I was pretty much out of it by the time I got down there.'

As they approached the village, most of the passengers walked towards the bow, ready to disembark. For Jack it might have brought back painful memories of his accident but, looking at Georgia, he could feel nothing but happiness about where his misfortune had led him.

Few passengers remained as the ferry departed. 'Look!' said Jack suddenly. Georgia followed his arm as he pointed out to sea. Shading her eyes, at first she saw nothing. Then a flying fish took off, followed by the rest of the shoal flitting and darting above the water in prodigious leaps before diving down and disappearing. It was enough to banish her disquiet and her spirits were further raised as the ferry approached the sparkling village of Loutro.

They cruised slowly past an island and a lighthouse into the semicircular bay with a tiny pebble beach. The bay was like a sheet of deep blue glass wrapped in the arms of the coastline on which teetered the village of white and blue houses, tavernas and small hotels. The ferry approached the quayside slowly, as though embarrassed to ruffle the tranquil surface of the water.

The clanking of the ramp being lowered was the only sound to disturb the silence as they disembarked. They let the peace engulf them as they explored the seafront before wandering through the narrow lanes of the tranquil village perched beneath the mountains. They walked as far as the beginning of a path which rose steeply, traversing the cliffs.

'That's the track to Chora Sfakion. It's about a seven kilometre trek. I've never done it myself,' admitted Georgia. 'I have been to Glyka Nera, Sweetwater Bay, by boat though, which is the other side of that headland,' she pointed. 'It's stunning. Cold, fresh water from the mountains bubbles up from under the sea bed. It's a strange sensation swimming there.'

Jack made a mental note to put it on his list of places to visit as they contentedly strolled back to the waterfront. On the edge of the beach, Georgia sat and slipped off her sandals. Jack sat down beside her and unlaced his shoes before they walked down to the water's edge letting the warm water wash over their feet. Jack would have liked to have reached out for her hand, but reticence got the better of him.

Sitting in a taverna, the rippling sea just inches away, they ordered mezzes for two and wine. Time seemed to stand still as they embraced the serenity, banishing all but their enjoyment of that moment.

The waiter brought fruit and raki to finish the meal and sitting back into the comfy chairs they toasted each other and the idyllic day that was unfolding.

'Where are you staying?' They heard the waiter ask as he put the bill on the table.

'Unfortunately we're not,' Jack replied. 'We'd love to but we're catching the ferry back to Paleochora.' Jack followed the waiter's eyes out to sea and watched the boat pulling away from the quayside. He had lost all track of time and knew the answer before he asked. 'There's not one later?' The waiter nodded his head, closing his eyes and tutted, confirming Jack's fears that they were stranded.

'Can we get a water taxi back?' Jack asked.

'To Paleochora. It would be very expensive. Why don't you stay overnight? I have a room available above the taverna.'

Jack looked across at Georgia, confusion on her face.

Georgia was suddenly panicked. Why had she let herself be lulled into a false sense of contentment? 'Oh no, we're not a couple,' she heard herself say.

Jack was shocked to see the change in Georgia. Minutes ago she had appeared relaxed in his company. Now all he could see was anxiety written across her features. He felt her reaction to the waiter's innocent suggestion like a slap in the face. 'It's OK; I don't mind paying for the water taxi. Would you be able to phone one for us?'

'Perhaps we could find somewhere with more than one room?' Georgia tried to retrieve the situation. She could see that her reaction had upset Jack.

'No, the water taxi will do fine,' Jack insisted. 'We can stay on a bit and explore while we wait. We might even catch the sunset on the way back, if that's alright with you?'

Georgia nodded her assent.

'Could we have another drink and maybe you could see if we can get the taxi for the early evening?' Jack asked the waiter who was relieved to disappear inside his taverna, leaving the pair sitting in awkward silence.

Jack felt the need to fill the void between them but could not find the words. Georgia's reaction to the idea that they might be a couple had filled him with a pain of rejection even without him declaring any romantic intentions. That she had made herself clear about her feelings so early on in their relationship sent his emotions spinning towards rock bottom.

Georgia could see that she had hurt him. 'I'm sorry. I got frightened that this was more than it is. It's just that since Rory's death and my breakdown I find it difficult to get close to anyone.' Jack watched as a tear rolled down Georgia's cheek. His instinct was to hug her but he thought better of it.

'The taxi's booked for six,' said the waiter, who appeared and put a jug of wine on the table.

'Thank you,' Jack said.

When they were alone again, Georgia continued. 'Every time I think I'm making progress, something happens and I feel anxious again.' She sobbed. 'I don't know what is wrong with me. I feel guilty that Rory died and I'm still alive. I feel guilty that I'm not working as a doctor and sometimes I get scared of the silliest things...'

Jack stood, rounded the table, bent down and encircled her in his arms. He felt her warm tears through his T-shirt as she wept, her body tense with anxiety. Slowly her tears began to dry and she began to relax a little. Jack went inside and paid the bill.

They meandered through the alleyways of the village, paddled in the sea and sat on the beach watching the boats in the bay. Even though full from lunch, Jack bought ice creams which they rushed to eat as the delicious scoops of vanilla and strawberry melted over their hands. By the time they stepped into the open boat that was to return them to Paleochora, Georgia had restored some equanimity. Numerous times she apologised to Jack and he swept her remorse aside, taking the time to listen when she felt the need to talk. He knew only too well the struggles she was having with her inner self.

It was still hot, and the breeze generated as the boat sped out to sea was welcome. The taxi moved close inshore traversing the mountainous coast, the cliffs casting cool shadows over the water. In what seemed like no time they were passing Agia Roumeli.

The skipper stared ahead as he steered the boat through the ultramarine waters, leaving behind a bubbling wake. Ashore, the long beach of Sougia unfolded in the last of the daylight as the sun burned orange above the horizon.

'Look!' shouted Georgia. Jack followed her gaze as the captain slowed the boat. Some fifty metres from the bow a dolphin broke the surface, followed by another. Spellbound, they must have counted ten frolicking in the sea. Jack looked at Georgia, her face lit up each time one of the pod jumped clear of the water, shrugging gleaming droplets from its glistening skin.

For several minutes the pod played, leaping and diving as though leading them home. Silhouetted by the orange sun as it dropped behind the promontory of Paleochora the last dolphin breached, and they were gone.

'That is one of the most beautiful things I have ever seen,' said Georgia, her face radiant. In the distance, lights were coming on in Paleochora, guiding them towards the town. Above them stars came out one by one as the sky darkened. Below, green phosphorescence sparkled, illuminating the sea.

The water taxi moored alongside the quay from which the ferry had departed that morning. Jack felt in his pack for his wallet and paid the fare. 'Let me pay some,' said Georgia, searching for some money. 'No. It was worth every penny, just to see the dolphins.' Jack held up his hand.

Georgia could see he was insistent. 'In that case I'll buy us a drink. I can get a taxi back to my grandmother's and pick up the car in the morning.'

'I'll take you up on that. The taverna where I'm staying is good, if you fancy that?'

In the town the tavernas were beginning to fill up as they walked through the narrow lanes. Behind walls in courtyards families sat talking, children playing in the streets as late season tourists browsed the shops for souvenirs.

'You found your friend then,' the taverna owner said to Jack as he showed them to a table outside on the crowded terrace beneath a pergola. 'How is your grandmother?'

'She's doing great, thank you,' Georgia replied. 'Sometimes I think she's got more energy than me.'

'Please, send her my regards.'

'Thank you, I will.' Georgia took the seat she had been shown to and Jack sat opposite and ordered two glasses of wine.

'I've enjoyed today,' said Georgia. 'Seeing the dolphins was magical. I'm sorry about…'

'Don't worry. I understand. And anyway, if we hadn't missed the ferry or we had stayed in Loutro we would never have seen the dolphins.'

'It's just that I'm not ready. In fact, I'm not sure I ever will be ready for another relationship. I'm a mess. When I lost Rory, I lost my best friend, my lover and eventually my job. I didn't mean to hurt you. When the taverna owner in Loutro suggested we stay together, it freaked me out. I mean, the thought that I was part of a couple...'

'You don't have to explain. I get it. I'm a bit of a mess myself if truth be told. Always have been, and this hasn't helped,' Jack nodded towards his leg. 'I came to Crete to try and get what there is of my career back on track, I'm heading for thirty and I can't forever keep relying on my parents to bail me out.'

'How long will you stay?' Georgia took a sip of wine.

'In Paleochora or Crete?'

'Both really.' Georgia leaned forward and for a moment caught Jack's eyes in hers.

'I think I'll head back to Elounda tomorrow, and I guess I'll stay there until I finish writing the book, on and off – these new regulations about how long you can stay make it more difficult.' He tried to make light of the decision he had made on the spur of that moment to return to the village. 'We can keep in touch. Come and visit if you like.' He realised how much he wanted her in his life. 'I could show you Spinalonga. I imagine it's changed a lot since you were last there. They've been restoring it. Stop me, I'm rambling…'

A smile lifted her mouth. 'I might just do that.'

*

Since Jack had left Paleochora, Georgia had found herself unable to call him. She had not exactly promised that she would, but she had led him to believe that there was a possibility she might join him in Elounda. What was stopping her? She had to admit she liked him. He was kind, handsome, and she felt comfortable with him. Since Rory's death, though, she had been unable to get close to anyone, scared that she might lose them and unsure of her self-worth after she had quit her career. Jack had his own challenges to deal with, he would be better off without her.

It was her grandmother who convinced her to make the call. 'What are you doing moping around the house?' she asked. 'Is it that young man?' Georgia had tried and failed to cover up her feelings and Maria encouraged her to talk about her fear of calling Jack. 'If you like him you should phone, what harm can it do? He seemed lovely, and you don't want to spend all your time with an old lady like me. Elounda is only at the other end of the island, not the other side of the world. What have you to lose?'

Georgia took out her phone, closed her eyes, opened them again, took a deep breath and pressed the number as her grandmother left the room.

Jack, who had given up hope that he would hear from Georgia, was delighted and surprised. She told him that if his offer was still open she would love to come and visit and to see the places she had been to in her childhood. She asked him when would be convenient.

'Come any time,' said Jack, 'and stay for as long as you want.'

'Would tomorrow be OK?' Georgia grasped the nettle, fearing her courage might ebb away.

'That would be great. You should be comfortable in the upstairs bedroom. If I'm honest my writing seems to have stalled a bit anyway,' Jack admitted. 'Perhaps visiting a few places with you will give it a kick start.'

When they hung up, Jack felt a rush of excitement. Since returning to Epano Elounda he had found himself unable to work. Each morning he would get up with the best of intentions, make himself a coffee and set up his laptop on the table on the terrace. He would try to make a start but anything but the words he was trying to write took his attention. He would stare down at the bay or the olive trees on the hillside. He would wave and greet neighbours walking in the village streets below. Now he had purpose, he began to tidy, clean and change the linen in the bedroom and make up the sofa bed for himself downstairs.

Georgia slipped her phone into the back pocket of her jeans. As she walked outside where her grandmother was sitting, she felt the anxiety that was never far away creep up on her.

'Did you speak to him?' Maria looked up.

'Have I done the right thing Granny? I said I'd go to Elounda tomorrow. I'll only stay a couple of days.'

'You stay as long as you like, darling. I'm fine here on my own. It'll do you good and, as I said before, Elounda's not the other end of the earth.'

Georgia went to her bedroom and packed and unpacked her case several times. How much and what should she take with her? She put in enough clothes for a couple of days. Jack might have a washing machine, and if not there was probably a launderette in Elounda.

She took the car to a garage and filled up with petrol before checking the tyre pressures and oil and water levels. She returned to the house and when she could think of nothing else to keep herself occupied, joined her grandmother on the terrace. Looking towards the sea, she saw nobody on the beach. A lone ship edged its way along the horizon heading east. She closed her eyes and listened to the water whispering as it caressed the pebbles on the shoreline. For several minutes the two women sat in silence, alone with their thoughts.

*

The following day Jack was up early. The house was clean and it was hours before he had agreed to meet Georgia at The Boatyard taverna. He got himself breakfast, but could hardly eat. He watered then dead-headed the plants on the terrace. He noticed a stain on top of the wall surrounding the balcony and tried to wash it off.

He looked at his watch. Time was still moving slowly. He decided he would walk to Elounda to take his mind off the wait. He had not attempted taking the old donkey track since he had broken his ankle. Parts of the path were uneven but he liked the challenge. He followed the narrow lanes downhill past Alexander's taverna. It was already hot and the cicadas had begun their chorus in the olive groves. He could see the bay shining blue, boats drawing filigree patterns of silver on the surface of the sea. The path crossed the new road which wound up the mountainside between dry stone walls enclosing smallholdings and olive groves. A lizard scuttled into a crack in the wall. The track was rocky and Jack had to keep his eyes on the ground to avoid falling. He heard the noise of children playing as the path emerged by a school and the going got easier as he found his way into the backstreets of Elounda. It was still only eleven o'clock, and Georgia was not due to arrive until around two.

On the quayside a fisherman was mending his nets, a cat asleep beneath the bench on which he sat. On the other side of the harbour wall he stepped down onto the beach, lively with weekend sunbathers and families swimming. Along the coast road he could see The Boatyard, Popi and Costas' caique at its mooring on the jetty. He sat on the sand and took off his shoes before paddling his way along the shoreline towards the taverna, enjoying the feel of the warm water.

He found his friends at a table outside drinking coffee and they were eager to hear his news. When they learned Jack had found Georgia and she was coming to visit they were delighted for him.

'You must bring her to meet us. What are you doing this evening?' Popi asked, looking at her husband. 'We could see you in Alexander's taverna for dinner, we've a trip this afternoon we have to get ready for but nothing booked after that.'

'I'm not sure Jack will want us with him on their first evening together,' said Costas.

'No, it's fine. That sounds great,' Jack thought the support of his friends might ease the nerves he was beginning to feel. 'Is nine OK for you?'

'We'll look forward to it,' Popi stood, and put a hand on his shoulder. 'Don't be so nervous,' she said reassuringly. 'See you this evening.'

As he watched his friends walk along the quay he looked at his watch. It was still nearly two hours before he had arranged to meet Georgia. He considered ordering a drink but thought better of it. A walk might settle his nerves.

On the harbour the fisherman had finished repairing his nets and was sitting smoking. He passed the row of ferries waiting their turn to transport passengers to Spinalonga. He took the narrow road alongside the seafront tavernas and cafés, stopping to chat with some of the owners and waiters. At the salt flats a grey heron was perched on a rock and Jack paused to watch.

At the top of the cobbled bridge which spanned the narrow canal he checked the time. The walk had taken longer than he thought. What if Georgia was early? As he strode at a good pace back past the salt flats, he saw the heron was still there, and heard a piano playing in the distance. Set back from the road he noticed a taverna, a sign announcing it as 'Sotiris' Piano Bar'. He was immediately drawn by the music but had to get on.

Hot and sweating, he arrived at The Boatyard, relieved to see that Georgia was not yet there. He sat down and ordered a beer. He looked at his phone to see if she had sent him a text. Nothing. Should he send her a message? No, she was only minutes late. Be patient, what was he worrying about?

Moments later he saw Georgia's car as she drove past searching for a parking space. He stood to watch as she found a spot, then waved as she approached. He could not help smiling at how beautiful she looked and how pleased he was to see her again. Her hair was tied back from her suntanned face that was lit up by the sparkling brown eyes and slight smile which greeted him.

'I'm sorry I'm a bit late. I set off really early so stopped in Agios Nikolaos to have a look around and got lost finding the road out.' Georgia held out her arms and gave him a hug before sitting down. 'I'd forgotten how beautiful it is here. The view as you come down the mountain is incredible.'

'Let me get you a drink. I've only just got here myself. What would you like?'

'I'll have a lemonade if that's OK? I'm sweltering after that drive. What a lovely taverna.'

'It belongs to the family of some friends of mine, Popi and Costas. Popi grew up in England, although she's Greek. She moved out here after her father died and left her a house in the village. It's a long story. I hope you don't mind but I've arranged for us to meet up with them in Epano Elounda later for a meal.'

'That sounds nice. I can't wait to see the house and the village.'

'We'll have these and then we can go and get you settled in, then you can relax.'

Georgia had to concentrate hard as she took the winding, steep, narrow road up the hillside. She wanted to soak up the view but was reluctant to take her eyes off the road. It only took minutes before Jack directed her into a parking space beside the church and he was pulling her case along a narrow footpath.

'Here we are.' Jack stopped in front of a blue front door and reached in his pocket for the key. Inside, the house was dark before Jack opened the windows and shutters, revealing the large, cool living room with a made-up sofa bed. Three steps led up to the kitchen and dining area off which Jack pointed out the bathroom. He picked up Georgia's case, carrying it up a flight of stairs.

'I hope this is OK? Your room is up here.' He put the case down and opened the door onto the terrace, flooding the upstairs with light. 'The bedroom is in there,' Jack indicated but for the moment Georgia could not resist the pull of the terrace and stepped into the sunshine. Entranced, she looked out over the higgledy-piggledy roofs of the village houses down the mountainside strewn with olive trees all the way to Elounda and the bay.

'Wow! That's quite some view,' Georgia gasped, 'I'm not surprised you find it difficult to write here. I would never be able to take my eyes off that.'

'It is difficult. My mum and dad were lucky to find the house, and I'm even luckier to be able to stay here. Why don't you make yourself comfortable. We've nothing to do until this evening. In the meantime I'll get us some snacks to tide us over.'

Georgia unpacked her case, then lay on the bed. It was so comfortable she could have fallen asleep there and then, but she was drawn back outside by the promise of the view and the food and drink that awaited her.

Jack pointed out the causeway and the quarry in the distance near Mochlos and the towering mountains stretching towards the far east of the island. He explained where Spinalonga was, the island hidden behind a ridge in the hillside. As her eyes took in the lie of the land it stirred a hazy recollection of her visit as a child. A cloud passed over her mind at the thought of those carefree days which had been lost to the events which now shaped her.

If not at ease, at least Georgia and Jack felt solace in each other's company. They knew the history of the events which had brought them here and were conscious of one another's emotional fragility. As they picked at olives and dipped bread in tapenade they sipped wine and the conversation skirted around each other's sensitivities. Jack got out his father's binoculars and they watched a large yacht anchoring in the Bay of Mirabello and a shepherd with his dog rounding up their flock on the hillside. A stray cat jumped onto the terrace from the roof next door and lay by Georgia's feet while Jack went to the fridge to find it some food. When he returned both were asleep. The cat woke up when he put down the bowl of food. He let Georgia snooze and went inside to get a book and read in companionable silence as she dozed. In no time Jack too had succumbed to the heat and closed his eyes.

'I'm so sorry. How rude of me.' Georgia woke to the sound of Jack's book falling on the floor. 'How long have I been asleep?'

'I don't know, I've been napping too.' Jack reached for his phone to see the time. 'Would you like a coffee, or tea? I'll get the kettle on.'

When Jack returned with the drinks the sun was beginning to sink beneath the mountains, the sky blazed red before giving way to a moonless inky blue dotted with stars. They sat in the darkness looking down at the lights of Elounda and the occasional fishing boat at anchor in the bay.

Popi and Costas were already seated in the taverna. Despite it being busy, Alexander left the grill, bringing raki and five glasses to the table, eager to meet Georgia. Introductions over with, the taverna owner returned to his cooking. Georgia and Popi were soon deep in conversation.

'Jack told me that you went to school and university in England,' said Georgia.

'That's right, I moved there after my parents split up when I was thirteen. I only returned when dad died five years ago. It seems a lot longer than that now. My mum moved back out here too and runs The Boatyard with her partner Andrew.' Popi went on to explain that Costas owned a boatbuilding business and when work was scarce was a sometime fisherman. They lived above the village in a house Popi had inherited from her dad.

The evening passed far too quickly. When Costas looked at his phone it was after one o'clock. The other customers had all left and Alexander was wiping down tables. 'We've nothing on tomorrow,' said Popi. 'How about we take you over to

Spinalonga and then head off along the coast? I'll do some lunch and we can make a day of it.'

Georgia looked at Jack and smiled.

'That sounds fantastic,' he said. 'Is there anything you want us to bring?'

'Just swimming gear and yourselves,' answered Popi.

'That's kind. I'd love that. I went as a child, but to be honest can remember very little about it,' said Georgia.

'They've done a fair bit of restoration work on it. Shall we meet up at our mooring at The Boatyard around eight thirty?'

Arrangements made, Jack insisted on paying the bill. They walked together up the lane, parting company at the door of Jack's house.

*

'What a beautiful boat,' Georgia said as she crossed the gangplank to board the *Katerina*.

'My father started building it and Costas finished it after he died,' Popi said proudly. 'It's named after my mum.' For the moment any conversation was drowned out as Popi turned on the engine while Costas hoisted the gangplank and cast off the stern line before weighing the bow anchor.

Popi set a course along the coastline towards the village of Plaka. The boat carved a path through the flat calm, leaving a trail of white across the perfect blue. Georgia watched as they motored past small beaches and large hotels and the occasional luxury villa before Popi headed across the bay towards the island.

'We'll drop you on the quay and then anchor up while you go round. Give us a ring when you've finished and we'll come and pick you up.' Popi directed the caique towards the jetty, holding it steady just long enough for Georgia and Jack to step ashore before reversing the boat away from the island.

They stood for a moment on the quayside looking at the gate through which the patients would have passed into their future lives on the island. They joined the short queue and paid the entrance fee before entering the village themselves through the tunnel which led through the fortified walls. Jack explained that this was called Dante's Gate, and that those who came this way would have had little expectation of ever leaving alive. Georgia felt a shiver pass through her as they stepped out into the sunlight on the inside of the ancient fortress.

'I can't remember any of this from when I visited as a kid.' Georgia stopped in front of an old taverna. 'I don't know what I expected but it makes sense that the people who were sent here tried to live as normal lives as possible.'

''In some ways it's life-affirming to know that they fell in love, married in the church here and had children,' said Jack.

They left the village behind and followed a path which led them to the seaward side of the island where beneath them lay the cemetery, the last resting place of those who had been exiled there. Looking down at the stark overgrown slabs which marked the tombs, Georgia could sense herself welling up as she was reminded of another more recent disease that had blighted the lives of so many. A tear ran down her face.

'Let's get out of here; Jack said, reaching for her arm and leading her up the hill towards the highest part of the island. Although out of breath they felt a sense of liberation as they climbed. Reaching the summit they looked down upon the forts built to guard the bay against invaders long before the island had been a leper colony. Anchored off the island they could make out the tiny figures of Popi and Costas sitting aboard *Katerina* awaiting their return.

'Shall we head down?' Jack pulled out his phone. 'I'll give Popi a ring and let her know we're on our way.'

Back aboard, Costas took the helm navigating between the island and rocky shallows to the open sea. Popi went below, returning with a tray of coffee and glasses of water, putting them on the cockpit table before going back to the cabin and emerging with a chart. 'This is where we are aiming to go to today,' she traced a course with her finger along the coastline.

'Can you see the quarry in the distance? We're heading across the Bay of Mirabello then around that headland past a place called Mochlos then further along the coast to the Richtis Gorge.'

Jack and Georgia followed Popi's pointing finger and could see in the distance the white scarring of the mountains where the rocks had been blasted to mine gypsum.

'I saw that from your terrace yesterday and wondered what it was,' said Georgia. 'It seems a long way away?'

'If we keep out to sea and head straight across the bay it's not that far. We thought if we anchor off the beach at the bottom of the gorge you two could walk up to the waterfall there. It's very beautiful and secluded it'll give you an appetite for lunch. It's a bit of a hidden treasure so we thought you might enjoy it.'

In the Bay of Mirabello a huge cruise ship like a floating block of flats waited as a tug approached to tow it into a berth on the quay. Costas steered quite close and Georgia shivered at the vastness of the vessel. Passengers lined the decks to watch the docking and some waved down at them. Georgia was relieved as Costas put more distance between *Katerina* and the monster ship. They felt the wash from the tug as it strained to edge the liner to shore. Ahead they could see rugged mountains which Costas identified for them as the Orno range.

'Look at the colour of the water,' Georgia exclaimed, tugging at Jack's arm.

Looking down, he could see the sea appeared an extraordinary mixture of green and light blue.

'Beautiful, isn't it?' said Popi. 'The freshwater springs from the mountains well up from the seabed and mix with water in the bay creating these amazing colours. And that island in front of us is called Psira, which means louse,' she explained. 'That tiny island tucked into the corner of the bay is called Konida, or nit, and round the headland near Mochlos is Psilos, the flea. Don't ask me why, probably something to do with their shape.' They steered towards the land and passed between Psira and the shore, seeing the sun reflecting off the windscreens of cars weaving their way along the national highway high above in the mountains.

'Does anybody live on the island?' asked Jack looking at Psira.

'It used to be a Minoan settlement, but was thought to have been overwhelmed by the massive tsunami which resulted from the earthquake which devastated Santorini around 1450 BC. The Romans built a lighthouse there, and the remains of a Byzantine monastery have been found but nobody lives there now. There are boat trips which go, and archaeologists are still excavating the ruins,' replied Popi.

Jack made a mental note to research the island further for his book. 'Wow, I didn't realise how massive the quarry was!' exclaimed Georgia as she turned her attention back to the shore and could see in front of them the vast open-cast gypsum mine stretching up the mountainside. Close inshore a freighter was moored at the end of a long quay which stretched out into the deep water. The quarry appeared to go on forever until they rounded a headland and the mountains returned to their natural terrain. Popi pointed out the tiny village of Mochlos and the small island of Psilos close to the shore. 'It's beautiful there and worth a visit. The sunsets are incredible. Just like an impressionist painting. It's a bit of a windy drive down from the main road, but well worth it.'

Beyond here the mountains took a step back from the sea leaving a narrow plain which was dotted with the occasional hotel and villas amongst the smallholdings where farmers made a living from the fertile soil. Tiny bays embraced secluded beaches. Around another headland the cliffs reasserted themselves, striding back to the shoreline, the waterfront rocky and strewn with giant boulders split from the mountains which towered above.

'There's a small beach at the bottom of the gorge, but it's too dangerous for us to get in too close. As it's so calm we'll anchor up and you can swim ashore. You can explore a bit of the gorge while we prepare the lunch and come back when you're ready.' Popi made her way to the bow and started to ready the anchor as Costas eased *Katerina* towards the deserted beach.

'I'm a bit worried about getting my leg wet.' Jack looked down at his prosthetic.

'Don't worry,' Costas opened a locker and pulled out a large dry bag. 'Put it in here and I'll follow you in to the beach with it. Put a couple of bottles of water and your T-shirts and towels in as well. When you get back, I'll come and pick it up again.'

The swim to the beach was not much more than twenty metres. Georgia sat next to Jack on a rock as he put on his leg and they carefully made their way up the beach towards the mouth of the gorge. 'I'll see you in a couple of hours or so. Just wave when you're back and I'll come and help you.' Costas shouted as he pushed himself back into the water and with a strong stroke headed back to the anchored boat.

They found the path into the gorge through an opening in the tamarisk trees that fringed the beach and followed the course of a stream, clear and cold and alive with small fish and freshwater crabs. 'Look, a peregrine falcon.' Jack pointed skywards to where the lone bird hovered above.

'This place is magical, like a secret garden.' Georgia pushed aside a branch which grew across the path. 'It's so humid here, like a tropical rainforest.'

They could hear the waterfall before they could see it but when they emerged in a clearing overhung by trees the sound of the water got louder as it plunged in ribbons fifty feet over a vertical rock face swathed in moss into a pool below. In the small clearing by the pool a wooden table had been placed.

'I'm sweltering, are you coming in?' Jack took off his T-shirt.

Georgia went over to the pool beneath the falls and dabbled a finger in the water. 'It's freezing.'

'It's supposed to be good for you. Come on!' Jack made his way to the pool, shivering as he edged his way in before committing and submerging his head. The cold punched the breath out of his body, Georgia had not been wrong.

'What's it like?' Georgia shouted.

'It's not too bad once you're in. Come on!' Jack watched as Georgia bent to slip off her shoes before pulling her T-shirt over her head. She wobbled her way over the uneven stones, screaming and laughing as she got deeper into the water before stumbling and falling into the pool. 'We must be mad, it's like ice!'

It didn't take long for their bodies to adjust to the cold. Jack felt for the bottom with his feet and stood. 'That was refreshing to say the least. Isn't this just perfect?'

Looking around at the water falling into the pool where she now stood, Georgia craned her head upwards towards the mountains from where the river had found its way and caught a glimpse of the clear blue sky above the verdant green forest and had to admit it was pretty much perfect.

'It's still cold though,' she replied.

'Let's get out.' Jack began to wade towards the edge of the pool. 'We should probably get back to the boat. I don't know about you, but I'm pretty hungry.'

As they emerged back onto the beach, Costas had already spotted them and dived off the boat to swim to shore and help them with the dry bag.

'It's not a bad spot, is it?' He asked his friends as Jack sat to take off his prosthetic.

'Thank you for bringing us here. It's beautiful,' replied Georgia.

'That's not what you were saying when you fell into the water at the pool,' laughed Jack.

Back aboard they dried themselves quickly, eager to tuck into the lamb stew, roast potatoes and stuffed peppers Popi had put out on the table in the cockpit. She went below and brought back some beers from the cool-box and they ate as the boat rocked gently on its anchor, the hint of the afternoon sea breeze ruffling the surface of the water.

Popi was keen to know how long her new friend would be staying in Elounda.

'It depends how long he'll have me,' Georgia grinned and turned to Jack. 'Have you got anything planned for tomorrow?'

'Maybe we could take a drive up to the Lassithi Plateau, if you fancy it? Shall we see how we feel in the morning?' Georgia was happy to go along with whatever Jack suggested.

By the time Costas weighed anchor and Popi had started the engine and headed back out to sea, Jack was already dozing. Georgia sat on the bench seat, holding on to the guardrail watching the small villages, rocky coves and sandy beaches on the shoreline as they retraced their way across the Bay of Mirabello. They passed Agios Nikolaos, the giant cruise liner moored up to the quayside. As they approached the island of Kalidon she thought she recognised the chapel of Analipsi on the headland from her visit as a child. She felt herself nodding off, and when she opened her eyes she saw they were passing through the narrow channel between Kalidon and Spinalonga, back into the Bay of Korfos.

The sun was going down over the mountains when Jack and Georgia said their goodbyes to Popi and Costas on the mooring and took the drive up the hillside to the village. Back in the house, Jack lit the candle lanterns on the terrace and put on some music.

'If it's OK with you I'll go and wash my hair?' Georgia asked.

'Of course. I'll get us some drinks and snacks.'

While Georgia was in the bathroom, Jack went to the kitchen and got out glasses and plates and took a bottle of wine from the fridge. He filled bowls with nuts and crisps, and plates with cheese, ham and biscuits which he took upstairs and laid out on the terrace table before pouring himself a drink. He sat back in a chair and closed his eyes. It had been a long time since he had felt so relaxed.

'I don't suppose you've got a hair dryer?' Georgia stood in the doorway wearing a blue cotton dress, her slim body framed by the light, her hair wrapped in a towel.

'My mum has one somewhere in the bedroom I think, probably in the bedside cabinet. I don't have much need for one myself.' Jack ran a hand over his head.

'Thanks, I'll take a look.'

Jack closed his eyes again and relaxed into his chair.

'I hope you don't mind but I took a peek at this.' Her hair still wrapped in the towel, Georgia pulled a seat next to Jack's and opened the photo album she was carrying. 'I found it in the cabinet. I hope you don't think I'm being nosy. Is that your mum and dad? What a beautiful couple.' Jack leaned over to look at the picture on the first page.

'Of course I don't mind. They're just old family photos of the first holiday we had here when I was a kid.'

Georgia flipped the page. 'It hasn't altered much.' She looked at pictures of the harbour and the church.

'Elounda might not have.' Jack unconsciously reached down and touched his prosthesis.

Georgia turned back to the album. She stared at a picture of a young boy standing on a beach holding a snorkel and mask. 'Is that you?'

'Haven't changed a bit.' Jack smiled.

'It's you! The boy who rescued my dolphin.'

The memory of the young girl standing on the beach by the causeway holding her father's hand flashed through Jack's mind.

*

'Catch it!' He had swum after the inflatable toy which had hit him, striking out with a strong crawl stroke but the wind was taking it away from him. He had been in luck, though: the zephyr disappeared as quickly as it had arisen and, as he approached, Jack had made out a blue and white dolphin bobbing on the water. He swung an arm over the toy, only for it to slip from his grasp. Catching it again he held it with both hands. Kicking his feet, he managed slowly to make it to shore.

Finding his footing in the shallow water, he had emerged from the sea. His arm was not long enough to encircle the toy and with the dolphin upright it was much taller than him.

'Thank you.' The man said, still holding the hand of his daughter. The girl was about his age, smiling self-consciously she stepped forward to reclaim her toy. She was taller than him, with long dark hair, brown eyes and a skin burnished by the sun. He glanced down at his own pale, skinny frame and managed to get out the words, 'That's OK,' as he handed over the dolphin. For a moment he held her smile before she turned and walked away, back to the beach on the other side of the causeway.

Jack's eyes followed her. For reasons he didn't understand he felt sad. Then he remembered the coin. As he got back into the water to begin what he knew would be a vain search for his treasure, he had had the strange feeling that he had lost something else.

As he suspected, he had no chance of recovering the coin. Even if he could have remembered exactly where he had dropped it, it would already have been covered by sand or hidden amongst the seaweed. For some time he had kept diving, before disappointment, tiredness and hunger got the better of him and he swam back to shore. On the beach he could see his parents, both asleep where he had left them. On the road he noticed a car pulling away, the head of an inflatable dolphin sticking out of the open sunroof.

*

Georgia leaned over and kissed him on the cheek. He turned his head and their lips touched and she pulled away.

'I'm sorry. I can't do this. It was my fault.' With tears suddenly welling in her eyes, Georgia stood and ran inside.

Jack sat rooted to the spot, his mind racing. Within minutes Georgia returned, her face red from the tears, holding her suitcase. 'I'd better go.'

Jack could think of no words, but in that moment of rejection realised that he loved her. 'Really, you don't have…' Georgia turned and walked towards the stairs. 'Let me carry your case.' But she was gone. Jack stood, unable to follow. He heard the front door close and her footsteps disappearing along the lane below into the darkness.

Chapter 10

2024

WHAT HAD SHE been thinking? Georgia drove at speed down the mountain road towards Elounda, trying to put as much distance as she could between herself and her misjudgement. Wiping back the tears, she threaded the car through the evening traffic, past the brightly lit shops, bars and tavernas. She accelerated up the mountain towards Agios Nikolaos. Looking straight ahead she kept her eye on the road but could sense the oily darkness of the sea beneath the cliffs.

If she didn't stop she would be in Paleochora around midnight. Back to the comfort of her *yiayia's* house. She welcomed the stretches of road works where she had to concentrate hard before the highway opened up and her mind would churn with thoughts of how she had kissed a man who in reality was little more than a stranger. She had told herself that after Rory's death she would not leave herself open to the pain of a relationship. What could anyone see in her, a needy, damaged woman who had failed in everything in her life? She had let her parents down when she left her job. She was bad news, only capable of hurting those around her. She switched on the windscreen wipers, but the mist she saw was in her head. Alarmed, she pulled off the road into a lay-by.

Fumbling for the handle, she opened the door. She was sweating. Leaning against the bonnet, she tried to slow her breathing. How long she stood there she did not know. Eventually she was able to stand and, taking deep breaths, got back into the car. She could not stay by the roadside all night; she had to get back to the safety of her grandmother's house. Georgia gingerly rejoined the road, driving slowly, gripping the wheel tight as she tried to pacify her thoughts.

Jack's head tumbled with confusion. The night that had sparkled with so much promise now appeared ominous. He tried to replay what had happened. He must have done something wrong, but was not sure what. Had he stupidly misread Georgia's friendly kiss on the cheek for something more than it was? Whatever had happened, she had gone. Why wouldn't she? What would a beautiful young doctor see in him, a no-hoper with one leg who was still living off his parents' generosity? Since coming to Crete, he had told himself he was writing a book, but what had he done? So far he had managed to break an ankle and spend time recovering, gone in search of a girl he had met briefly at university and upset her and, as for the book and making a living, not one page had been written. He reached out for the bottle on the table and poured himself another drink.

Jack felt a chill and woke up. He was still on his chair on the balcony. He did not have to look at the wine bottle to know that it was empty. The memories of the evening came back and he felt himself spiralling into the depression with which he was all too familiar. He forced himself to stand up. He went inside to seek the refuge of his bed.

It was midnight by the time Georgia turned onto the road south through the foothills of the shadowy White Mountains. She had to concentrate hard in the darkness. Her body tense, she was exhausted. All she wanted to do was get to bed and sleep.

She drove slowly over the path leading to her grandmother's house, tyres crunching the pebbles. She crept to the door and felt for the lock. Before she could turn the key, the door opened.

'I heard you coming up the drive.' Her grandmother stood aside, holding the door open. 'What on earth are you doing coming home at this time of night?' Maria could see her granddaughter was distressed and put an arm around her shoulder, ushering her inside. Whether it was the emotional turmoil or relief to be safely back at her *yiayia's*, Georgia's face crumpled and she began to cry.

'Let's get you to bed. You must be exhausted. You can tell me all about it in the morning.'

*

Even in the darkness, Jack knew from the heat that it was late. If he didn't make himself get up he would only wallow in the thoughts that consumed him. Opening the windows and blinds, he blinked as sunlight bathed the room.

He forced himself to shower, then sat on the terrace. He did not feel like eating and even the view could not shake the memory of the previous evening. He willed himself to leave the house and set off towards the donkey track and Elounda. The walk, which on so many a day had lifted his spirits, did little to lighten his depression. He was not concentrating on where he was walking and tripped and nearly fell on the cobbles. He made himself stop and sat on a drystone wall, wiping the sweat from his face on his T-shirt. He took out his phone and found the photo he had taken in Topsham and then the more recent shots of Georgia and himself on their trip to Loutro.

He resumed his walk, this time taking more care of his steps. Reaching the square he sat on a bench, watching the boats and the people walking by but he could not shake thoughts of Georgia. Of course he knew where she lived, but from the way she had left so abruptly he was sure she did not want to see him. More in hope than expectation he pulled his phone from his pocket and tapped in, 'Just wanted to check if you're OK? I'm sorry for whatever happened.' He hadn't been sure what to write but was concerned for Georgia. As he suspected, his message went unanswered. He walked along the harbour front to the beach. On the bay he could see Popi's caique approaching the pier near The Boatyard, a group of passengers getting ready to disembark. He felt the need to talk and headed for the taverna.

Jack approached as his friends were walking up the quay. He tried to disguise his feelings but he knew his face gave his sadness away.

'Hey, what's the matter with you?' said Popi, concerned. 'Where's Georgia?'

'She's gone,' was all Jack could say.

'Let's go inside. Do you want to talk about it?' Popi put an arm around his shoulder.

Jack was not sure what there was to say but let himself be led inside the taverna.

'Would you like a drink?' Costas offered.

'I think I probably had enough last night, I'll have a coffee if that's OK.'

At first, Jack was reluctant to speak about what he understood so little himself. But as he began to open up, he found some relief in sharing what had happened the night before. How Georgia had kissed him on the cheek and then... He didn't know what had happened, had he tried to kiss her or had it been an accident? Whatever the reason, he had frightened off the woman he had only just realised he was falling in love with.

'Have you told her how you feel?' asked Popi.

'I don't think that would make any difference, I think she made her feelings clear last night. And you can understand why she wouldn't want to be with me,' Jack added. 'It's best I just forget her.'

'That's not true. We could see that she really liked you,' said Popi.

'Well, it's too late now,' Jack tried to move the conversation on.

But Popi would not let it go. 'You've got her phone number, haven't you? Ring her.'

'I might do later,' said Jack to placate his insistent friend, but had no intention of calling Georgia and facing the pain of the rejection that was bound to follow.

'I don't think I'm very good company at the moment.' Jack drained his coffee and got up to leave.

Popi and Costas could see their friend wanted to be alone and made no attempt to stop him. 'Ring her,' Popi repeated as Jack left the taverna.

He headed back along the beach to the square, not noticing the friendly greetings of the locals who recognised him as he walked past, his eyes cast downwards. He walked beside the bay towards the bridge but the view of the waterfront no longer sparkled and the sun on his back didn't warm his soul.

He decided to turn back. Returning to the harbour he took a taxi from the rank to the church in Epano Elounda and traipsed along the overgrown path to the house, stepped inside and closed the door behind him.

As the day wore on, though, he thought about what Popi had said. What had he to lose by making the call? What difference would another humiliation make to his already rock-bottom mood? When he got back to the house he punched in Georgia's number. He let it ring for some time. There was no reply. He left it for five minutes and tried again and his call went straight to voicemail. He needed no further confirmation that she didn't want to speak to him.

*

'I've made you a cup of coffee.' As Georgia stirred she heard her grandmother enter the room and put a cup down on the bedside table.

'What time is it?' she asked.

'I thought I'd let you sleep after your late night. It's nearly midday,' Maria answered. 'Would you like me to make you some breakfast?'

Georgia's head was already awash with recollections of the night before. 'I'm not really hungry, granny.' Georgia swung her legs out of bed and put her head in her hands.

'You get up and have a shower. I'll make you something, you've got to eat.'

Reluctantly Georgia did as she was told, got to her feet and made her way to the bathroom.

The hot water did little to revive her spirits as she stared at it spiralling down the drain. She remembered the events of the previous evening and felt her body begin to stiffen with anxiety. She did not know what had come over her when she had kissed

Jack on the cheek and then on the lips. The fear that she felt now was only slightly diminished by the distance between them. She felt the tears welling up, and watched as they mingled with the water in the shower tray. When she'd seen the photo of Jack as a boy, it brought back memories of the years when she had been happy. But that was long ago, before Covid, the death of Rory and the loss of her career. Now she was so afraid of everything that she was barely living. She thought she had been making progress but a moment of stupidity had set her back again.

The table was laid with coffee, water, yoghurt, fruit and a croissant. As Georgia stepped outside, Maria could see she had been crying. 'Do you want to talk about it?' She took Georgia's hand, and listened as her granddaughter related what had happened in Elounda.

Maria let Georgia talk. She was patient and attentive as the words spilled out, words revealing her deep-rooted fear of getting close to anyone. 'And do you think you love Jack?' her grandmother asked.

'It really doesn't matter what I feel. There's no way he would want me.'

'Now, that is nonsense.' Maria said kindly. 'He came all the way to Paleochora to find you after seeing you in the gorge. He invited you to Elounda. Why on earth would he do that if he didn't like you?'

Georgia let her grandmother's words sink in. 'Well, even if he did, he won't now. I'd only hurt him. Why do I always mess things up?'

'You never told me how you two met. Have you been friends for long?' Maria asked.

'Well, until yesterday, I thought the first time we had met was at university, but then it was only on the night before we both left. I hadn't seen him again until the other week.'

'You said thought,' Maria raised an eyebrow.

'I found a photo album at his house. In it was a picture of a boy who had rescued my beach toy, a dolphin, from blowing away, that day when Mum and Dad took me to visit Elounda and Spinalonga when I was a young girl. I don't know what came over me, and I kissed him.' Georgia looked downwards.

'*Moira*, fate,' Georgia was sure she heard her *yiayia* whisper as she told the story. 'All is not lost. You have his phone number? You can always ring him.' At that moment Georgia's phone rang. She glanced at it and looked up. Aren't you going to answer that?'

Jack's name came up on the screen. Answering the call was the last thing Georgia wanted to do. 'It's nobody I know.' She let the phone ring out then switched it straight to voicemail.

*

Jack could not shrug off the pain of being rejected. At night he found sleep elusive. During the day he tried to take up his neglected writing. He was listless and spent the days walking aimlessly around Elounda making regular stops to drink and eating little. In the evenings he would go to the local taverna but if he ordered food he picked at his plate.

It had been a week since Georgia had run out on Jack when Popi and Costas saw him in The Boatyard. He looked dishevelled and tired as they asked if he minded if they join him for a drink.

'I'm not very good company at the moment.'

The couple sat down anyway, concerned for their friend's wellbeing. He told them that Georgia hadn't answered or returned his calls and that he was trying to forget her.

'You can't go on like this,' Costas told his friend.

'I know, but I'm going nowhere staying here. I need to get away, back to England. Perhaps that would help put all this behind me.'

'Have you written to her? Told her how you feel,' Popi suggested.

'I don't have her address,' Jack pushed the idea aside.

'You can message her, you've got her number. Tell her how you feel. At least if you do that you know you've tried and can get on with your life, either here or in England.'

Jack was reluctant to even consider the suggestion. Georgia was refusing to answer his calls and obviously wanted nothing to do with him.

But alone that afternoon, the idea began to hold more sway. He had nothing to lose. He tried to compose a text on his phone, but the right words were elusive. He went inside and found a notebook and pen and began writing and rewriting, crossing out and editing until he had found the words which expressed how he felt. Although Jack was not sure what had happened the evening she left, he apologised again. He told her that he thought he was falling for her and although he knew she was unlikely to feel the same way, he had to tell her how he felt or he would regret it for the rest of his life. If there was a chance she had any feelings for him they should meet up again, either in Paleochora or in Elounda. He agonised over finding the right words before copying them onto his phone and pressing send.

*

Georgia heard her phone vibrate on the table. 'Aren't you going to read that?' Maria asked. Georgia glanced at the screen. 'Why don't you see what he has to say?'

Georgia gave up any pretence that it was not Jack and reluctantly picked up her mobile.

Her grandmother saw her eyes widen as she read the message. 'Well, what does he say?' Georgia passed her phone across the table.

'So much for him not wanting anything to do with you.'

'What do you think I should do?'

'That is up to you, but one thing I do know is that if you like him you should give him a chance. You can't do his thinking for him. Not everyone has as low an opinion of you as you have of yourself. You can't keep running away from doing things just in case they don't work out. Phone him and arrange to meet up.'

Georgia could not bring herself to make the call, but was persuaded to send a message. In it she apologised to Jack for walking out on him and reiterated how she was frightened of any relationship, but said that she would like to meet up with him again.

*

When Jack's phone vibrated, it took him some minutes before he could bring himself to look at the message. He steeled himself for rejection, and had to read Georgia's text several times before it sunk in. He responded, asking where and when they should see each other. Both of them were keen to meet as soon as possible before the fear set in and they found excuses to avoid the encounter. Georgia insisted that she would drive to Elounda. She thought it best that they get together somewhere that would not stir memories of the evening she had walked out. Jack suggested they meet at The Boatyard the following day at two.

Jack was apprehensive and elated all at the same time. He wanted to share his news with someone. It was Popi and Costas who had encouraged him to send the text so he called their number. They were out on the boat, returning from an evening cruise.

'Why don't you come down for a drink? We should be in by the time you get here and you can tell us all about it.'

Jack looked over the balcony and thought he could see the navigation lights of *Katerina* out in the bay. It was too dark to take the donkey track, so he stuck to the road which wound down the mountainside. By the time he arrived at the taverna his friends were already at a table and a beer awaited him. They were pleased to see him happier and bursting with the news that Georgia was coming the following day. But his excitement was tinged with anxiety about them meeting up again and what they would do to alleviate any awkwardness.

Popi said, 'Look, if you don't mind having me around we could go out on the caique. Costas has a meeting tomorrow with a potential client about building a boat, so I'm at a loose end. I could make us all a meal and we could go swimming. It might help break the ice?'

Jack could feel the relief at the idea. 'I think we would both feel more comfortable. I'll text now and ask her to bring her swimming stuff.'

*

Georgia had already packed and was about to go to bed when the message came through. The suggestion that they would go out on the boat and go swimming calmed some of her nerves and she responded to Jack's message with a smiley icon before putting her swimming costume in the case and going to bed.

Her head flip-flopped between excitement and anxiety at seeing Jack again, and she found it difficult to sleep. She was now embarrassed by her hasty departure from Elounda. He had said in his text that he thought he might be falling in love with her.

Despite a restless night, she awoke early feeling strangely refreshed. She tried to move quietly around the house but her grandmother was already up and made her a coffee and breakfast.

If she set off now, she knew she would be early for the time she had agreed to meet Jack, but she was too distracted to keep up a conversation with her grandmother and was just killing time. 'Why don't you get off,' Maria suggested. 'You can always stop for a coffee on the way.'

Maria hugged her granddaughter through the open car window, and waved as she drove away along the pebble drive across the beach. The day was full of promise and Georgia felt an unfamiliar sense of wellbeing as she drove through the outskirts of the town and joined the road lined with polytunnels and greenhouses before an avenue of eucalyptus trees led her from the peninsula into the mountains and the olive-laden valley of Kandanos.

It was more than an hour before she turned east onto the national highway along the north coast of the island. Near Rethymnon she took her grandmother's advice and pulled over for a coffee. Past the ancient city, the road flirted with the coast, clinging to the cliffs before diving inland and weaving around the hillsides. Georgia had plenty of time. She was determined not to be intimidated by the cars and lorries impatient to speed past her. She wanted to enjoy the journey and appreciate the spectacular surroundings. The road weaved its way towards Heraklion, traversing the hillsides. To her left, far below the road, the infinite blue sea stretched away to where it hazily fused with the sky.

Rounding a sharp bend, a car sped towards her, overtaking a truck. In her mirror she saw the car behind pull out to pass her. There was no way it would make it in time. Georgia braked hard, wrestling her vehicle across the solid white line on the edge of the road to give more room for the overtaking car.

The sound of horns blared as the car cut in front of Georgia, narrowly missing her before losing control and crashing into the barrier, spinning across to the other side of the road, then through the rails.

Georgia sat motionless in her seat. Vehicles were stopping. She looked to where steam was rising from below where the car had crashed through the barrier. She opened her door and ran towards it. The vehicle had not plunged into the sea as she had feared but had come to rest upside down, wedged by a tree just before the hillside turned into a sheer cliff, falling away to the water below. She passed through the smashed barrier and reached in a pocket for her phone. Losing her footing on the loose stones she stumbled, dropping her mobile as she reached out to steady herself. She watched, helpless, as her phone hit a rock and rolled over the cliff top towards the water far below.

A small crowd was already gathering. Georgia looked up.

'Someone phone an ambulance and the police, and probably the fire service too,' she shouted. Turning, she edged her way towards the stricken car.

She heard someone shout, 'Careful, don't go down there!'

Then she recognised her own voice replying, 'I'm a doctor,' as she reached the upturned vehicle.

Remarkably the driver was still conscious, with some cuts to his face. The airbag had inflated and the man had pain in his ribs. Georgia would have preferred to have waited for assistance before getting him out of the car, but the injured driver was panicking as he saw his precarious position and pleaded to be helped out. She had been joined by two men who had edged their way down the hillside towards the top of the cliff and who helped prise the door open before one of them reached in and unclipped the seat belt and the man was extracted from the crumpled vehicle.

In the distance she heard a siren. The injured man was helped to safe ground and laid down. While Georgia tended to him as best she could, the emergency services began to arrive. He looked to have broken ribs and abrasions to the face but Georgia explained her concerns about internal bleeding and concussion to the paramedics who took over his treatment and transferred him to the ambulance. Georgia was then ushered to a police car where she was asked to give a statement about the accident.

It was warm in the car but Georgia was feeling cold and clammy, and her head began to spin. Concerned, the policeman shouted for the paramedics.

'I think you might be in shock, it's probably best if you come to hospital too and get checked out,' said the ambulance man.

'But I'm due to meet someone in Elounda,' Georgia pleaded.

'There's no way we can let you drive in that condition,' the policeman said kindly. 'Look, you go in the ambulance, and we'll get your car to the police station in Heraklion. Then, when you're given the all clear, you can pick it up there.'

There was no use protesting. In her heart Georgia knew that she was in no state to drive. The paramedic led her to the ambulance, following her inside and closing the door.

Chapter 11

2024

JACK ARRIVED EARLY at The Boatyard. Sitting at a table outside, he watched as Popi turned up and unloaded two large cool-boxes from her car and put them aboard her caique before joining him. Jack kept looking at his watch. At first Popi chided him for his impatience. Two o'clock came and went, and she had to reassure him that Georgia must have been held up on the road. An hour later, there was still no sign of her.

'Should I call?' Jack asked his friend.

'Give it a bit. It's only an hour. I'm sure she'll be here soon,' Popi said supportively, but she could see Jack's mood begin to dip.

After two hours even Popi's optimism was wearing thin. 'Perhaps you should try her?'

Nervously Jack dialled the number. The phone went straight to voicemail. 'She's not coming. I knew she would change her mind. Why wouldn't she?'

'Give her a bit longer; maybe she's got no signal.'

Jack put his phone down on the table. Minutes later he picked it up and redialled. Then he called again, and again.

Popi could see that her friend was getting agitated. 'Maybe she's broken down or had a puncture.'

'She would have called, or at least messaged me. She's not coming. I can't do this anymore.' Jack stood.

'Where are you going?'

'Home, on the first flight I can get out of here!' He was out of earshot by the time Popi could think of any words to stop him. Open-mouthed, she watched as Jack got into his car, slammed the door and drove off at speed.

*

Popi had been too shocked to try and stop Jack from leaving. She had been sure that Georgia would turn up and had been convinced that both of them had strong feelings for each other. Despondent, she could not shake her mood and spent the afternoon hanging around her mother's taverna drinking coffee and helping clear tables.

As the afternoon drew to a close, Popi was preparing to unload the cool-boxes from the cockpit of the caique when she noticed the white car park outside The Boathouse. She hurried over to the taverna. Georgia was desperately looking around and seemed relieved when she saw Popi approaching.

'I'm so sorry I'm so late,' Georgia blurted. 'There was an accident…'

'Slow down. Take a seat,' Popi said. 'Are you alright? That's the most important thing.'

'I was a bit shaken up, but I feel a lot better now. A car went through a crash barrier. I stopped to help. Then the police wouldn't let me drive...' She could hear herself babbling. 'Where's Jack?' Georgia was asking the question Popi had been dreading.

'He's gone home,' she answered.

Georgia made to stand up. 'I'd better drive up to his house and apologise. I dropped my phone and couldn't…'

'No. He's gone home. To England.' Popi thought it was best to come straight out with it. 'He thought you'd stood him up and was upset. He went to the village to pack his stuff and book a flight hours ago. I've tried to phone him but he's not answering.'

Popi saw Georgia trying to hold back the tears and wrapped her arms around her. She let Georgia sob on her shoulder until the crying subsided.

'I'm sorry,' Georgia whispered, lifting her head. 'Everyone's looking at us.'

'Don't worry about them. Would you like to go somewhere private and talk? I've still got the food I prepared and drinks if you'd like to come out on the boat and tell me about it.'

'I'm not hungry. But I could do with the company. I don't feel like driving back to Paleochora tonight.'

'Don't even think about it,' Popi insisted. 'You can stay at ours. 'Come on, the boat will be a good place to chat.'

Taking Georgia's hand, she helped her aboard before casting off the stern line. When she turned the ignition, the engine sprang to life and Popi went forward, quickly writing a text to Jack into her phone, although she suspected his flight had already taken off. She weighed the anchor and returned to the cockpit to take the tiller.

The sun glowed orange, making its descent toward the mountains. The sea gleamed silver as a hint of breeze rustled the darkening surface. The two women sat in silence, Georgia contemplating the events of the afternoon and how they had so cruelly conspired to keep her and Jack apart. It was only now, when she realised he had gone, that she felt the full strength of her feelings for him. Georgia felt herself shiver, and wished she had taken her case from the car.

'Hold this straight for a moment,' Popi indicated the tiller. 'I've got a warm jacket you can wear.'

Georgia gripped the helm tight, holding a course ahead as Popi disappeared below to the cabin, emerging with a coat, putting it around her friend's shoulders before taking back control of the caique.

In the distance Georgia recognised the honey-coloured buildings on Spinalonga dappled in the last of the evening sunlight. There were no boats moored off the island now, the last of the tourists gone for the day. Popi steered the caique across the bay passing a small boat fishing off Kalidon, before turning in the direction of the canal, skirting the island. Ahead Georgia could see the curve of the causeway. A gust of wind brushed her face and she was grateful for the jacket. Rising from the rocky shoreline, in the fading light she could make out the drystone walls running up the scrubby hillsides and a goatherd's shelter. A car drove across the bridge over the canal and onto the track which hugged the coast of Kalidon.

'Damn!'

Georgia turned to look at Popi as she heard her swear and cut the engine.

'We've got something tangled around the prop. It must have been just beneath the surface and I didn't see it. I'll drop the anchor and get a knife to cut us free.'

Popi stepped onto the deck and felt the boat lurch beneath her feet. In a second she realised they were moving backwards, towards the rocks.

The tail fin of a dolphin broke the water, thrashing furiously.

The boat was being pulled towards the rocks by the distressed creature.

Georgia was instantly on her feet. 'Get me the knife. You sort the anchor,' she shouted, tugging her dress over her head.

Popi got the sheaf knife from the cockpit and handed it to her. Knife in hand Georgia dived off the stern as Popi dropped the anchor from the bow.

In the low light it took some moments for her eyes to adjust and Georgia wished she had been wearing a mask. She felt the tension in the rope held tight by the dolphin struggling behind her and grabbed the line and cut through it. She could hold her breath no longer. Georgia surfaced and took a gulp of air.

She could make out the rocks below. Georgia inhaled and dived again, feeling along the rope for where it was tangled around the propeller. Holding the line with one hand she sawed at the knotted rope. Her lungs were burning. She closed her eyes and with one last pull on the knife felt the rope part. She kicked for the surface and breathed.

'Keep clear!' Gasping, she heard Popi shouting, 'I'm starting the engine.'

Georgia swam away from the boat and turned on her back, floating. She heard the muffled rumble of the engine and felt the water churning just metres away from her before the caique began to move towards the safety of deeper water.

Taking in some deep breaths Georgia turned and swam towards the shore. She could make out the water stirring and caught glimpses of the stricken dolphin's tail fin breaking the surface. Knife still in hand, she kicked towards the shallower water.

*

Jack stared at the bridge and out across the vastness of the Bay of Mirabello. He watched as the streetlights came on across the causeway, He did not know how long he had been sitting there, his thoughts in turmoil, his body exhausted. He did not know what had changed his mind. If he had bought a ticket, he would now be on his way back to England, to the safety of his parents' home and all the support he knew that would bring.

Something had stopped him. He was tired of running away, of not facing his fears. He had to find a way of cutting a path in this world. He had friends in Elounda. Probably more real friends than he had in England. He had somewhere to live and, if he could find the right motivation, the time to write.

From where he sat on a rock, he could see the small beach he recalled from his first visit here as a child. He saw the navigation lights marking the channel which led to the canal passing under the bridge and into the Bay of Korfos. He stared at the calm waters close to the causeway. Beneath lay the sunken city. He remembered the coin he had found, on one side a dolphin, on the other face the goddess Britomartis. He had lost the coin, and now he felt the pain return as he thought about how he had lost the girl he had first set eyes on here all those years ago. He thought about driving back to Elounda to get a drink, but felt tiredness consume him. He set off along the track to where he had parked his car near the bridge.

In the distance, on Korfos, he could see the green, white and red lights of a boat. Maybe a fisherman out to set his nets. As he got nearer, he heard a shout drifting in on the breeze. One woman's voice and then another. He stared at the caique and recognised the boat and the voices. On the foredeck he saw Popi wrestling with the anchor as someone dived off the stern into the water. The caique was moving dangerously close to the shore. He started running.

Before he could get close to the boat he heard the sound of the engine starting and saw Georgia surface the water. A wave of relief washed over him and he stopped to collect his thoughts. She had come.

*

Close up, the distressed dolphin was large and its frantic attempts to escape the net made Georgia fearful. At first she kept her distance, then took a deep breath and dived. Through the water, Georgia heard the dolphin's frightened whistles. She had to catch another breath. She found the surface and gulped in the air.

'Don't be afraid,' she whispered to the dolphin, and dived again. Adrenaline coursed through her and she no longer felt any fear. She reached out for the dolphin's nose around which the net was wrapped. To her surprise, at her touch the creature stopped struggling, as though it sensed she would help. She would have to clear the rope entirely or it would not be able to feed. She felt as though time had slowed down as she sawed through the cords. Her chest was bursting as the last strand parted and she kicked for the surface and inhaled the air.

Gasping, she felt something skim her leg. Opening her eyes she saw the dolphin, free of the net, break the surface just metres from where she was treading water. She allowed herself a smile as she watched the tail fin disappear beneath the surface.

She lay on her back. Above her a shooting star arched across the dark blue sky. Through the water she was sure she heard a whistle, and then another. Lifting her head she saw the dolphin breach and then beside it another emerged before both dived and disappeared into the bay.

'Thank God you're OK.'

Georgia turned at Jack's voice and saw him swimming towards her. She felt his arms wrap around her and could feel the tears welling up, but this time they were tears of happiness. She put her arms around his neck and kissed him.

Epilogue

2025

GEORGIA COULD HEAR Jack pacing about inside the house.

'Relax!' she shouted from the terrace. 'You know what flying is like, they'll get here eventually. We can go up to the vineyard if you like. Text your parents and tell them to meet us there. I don't mind driving, but we could walk up, it would kill a bit of time and might calm you down. My mum has just messaged to say they are on their way with granny and have just gone past Heraklion and will be here in about an hour.'

Closing the door behind them, they set off to the top of the village where the lanes gave way to a steep path up the mountain through the olive groves. Every now and then they would stop and look back over the terracotta rooftops of the village and down to the bay before continuing their way to the restaurant at the vineyard where the party was to be held.

The owners Chloe and Thanos were laying out tables on the large terrace which looked out over the neat rows of vines which they tended, and the winery, the products of which were gaining an increasingly good reputation.

Thanos looked at his watch. 'You're early.'

'Sorry, I hope you don't mind,' apologised Georgia. 'He was driving me mad pacing up and down in the house. Can we help you set up?'

'We're pretty much there, I think,' replied Thanos. 'Phoebe and Alice should be here soon to set up the sound system for the music. I think Alexander is going to play lyra with them. But apart from that we're all ready. The chef's OK in the kitchen, he won't need my help until the guests start to arrive and it's only forty or so people.'

Jack's head was spinning with an uneasy cocktail of nerves and excitement. He kept walking over to the wall surrounding the terrace to peer down at the road from Elounda. Several cars passed by on their way up to the remote mountain villages before one pulled into the gravel drive of the taverna and his mother and father got out.

Georgia hurried to greet them. 'Thank God you've arrived,' she laughed, hugging them both in turn. 'I thought Jack was going to burst if he had to wait much longer.'

Jack stepped forward and hugged his parents, 'Did you have a good flight?'

'Delayed a bit taking off from Gatwick. Air traffic control.' His father opened the boot and took out a package and offered it up to Jack. 'We dropped our luggage off at the house on our way up. Here's what you've been waiting for.'

Jack stepped forward and took the package, trying not to look too eager. He put it down on a table beside him. 'Go on, open it,' Georgia said. 'You know you can't wait.' Taking a knife from the table she held it out to him. Jack ran it along the tape sealing the top of the box, opened it and removed the bubble wrap before lifting out one of the pristine copies of his book. For a moment he stared at the cover before flipping through the pages inside. He could not keep the smile from his face as he handed it to Georgia and took out another two copies for his father and mother to see.

'Congratulations, it looks great,' his father turned the book over in his hands. 'You should be very proud of it. I know I am of you.'

'We all are, darling,' said his mother giving him a hug.

Georgia kissed him. 'Well done. It looks fantastic.'

Jack felt a tear come to his eye. 'Well, shall we get a drink to celebrate before the other guests arrive? I think there's a bottle of champagne on ice somewhere.'

As Jack walked towards the taverna he felt elated. There had been times when he never thought this day would come. It occurred to him that he felt truly happy. He was with the woman he loved and at last had achieved the success of writing a book. Of course, nobody had bought it yet, but just seeing it in print was an achievement in itself.

He reflected on how he had given up on writing a travel book and, at Georgia's suggestion, decided to try a novel. At first he had been unsure, but found the freedom to let his imagination run suited him, and since his new-found contentment with Georgia he had discovered the enthusiasm to sit and write each day. Every morning when he was in Crete, she would get up and leave him to work while she walked down the donkey track to the bay to swim.

The road to publication had been bumpy; he found it difficult to work in England, where he had to return regularly to satisfy residency regulations, and at times he had felt like giving up; but with Georgia's support and the encouragement of his parents he had finally made it. Georgia too had found the fortitude to return to her career. Saving the stricken driver on the cliff and rescuing the dolphin had proved to her that she had rediscovered the strength it took to save lives, and she had got a job working in the hospital in Agios Nikolaos whilst studying online for a master's degree in psychology from her old university, Exeter.

When it had been suggested, Jack had shied away from the idea of a launch party and even a book signing in London but had been persuaded to have a gathering of his friends and family in Crete to celebrate his achievement.

'I'll bring this,' Chloe said, picking up a tray with four glasses. 'Can you take the champagne?' Jack picked up an ice bucket with a bottle in it and followed Chloe back outside. 'You deserve it.'

Chloe handed out the glasses, popped the cork and poured each of them a drink.

'A toast.' Stephen raised his glass. 'To *On Dolphin Bay*. May it bring you every success.'

Jack held up his glass and thought how it already had, and how his life had changed so much over the previous year. He cradled his drink and walked across the terrace, allowing himself a moment of solitude. A hand touched his shoulder, and he turned to see Georgia.

'The guests are starting to come,' she said and he followed her eyes towards the cars approaching up the mountain road. Before they arrive, I wanted to give you this.' Georgia handed him a small decorative bag, inside which was a gift-wrapped present. Jack carefully untied the bow and took off the paper revealing a box. Opening the lid, he took out a chain with a silver pendant.

'I had a friend in Paleochora make it specially.' Georgia smiled as Jack turned the pendant over in his hand. On one side a dolphin, on the other Britomartis. A replica of the coin from the sunken city he had found and lost as a boy. 'This way you will never lose it again.'

Georgia could see that Jack was overcome with emotion. 'Come on, people are here,' she grabbed his elbow.

'No, not yet.' Jack pulled his arm away. 'I have something for you too. I was going to wait until later but…'

She saw Jack fumbling in his pocket before opening a box and presenting her with a beautiful solitaire diamond ring. 'Will you marry me?'

'Yes. Yes.' Georgia had never been more certain of anything in her life as she hugged Jack and kissed him. 'I have another piece of news,' Georgia whispered in his ear. 'We're going to be parents.'

If Jack had thought he could not have been happier, now he was almost overwhelmed with elation. He took a step back and looked at Georgia's face beaming with joy.

'Are you sure?' he asked her.

'I am a doctor,' Georgia said, laughing.

'Yes, you are.' Jack put his arm around her waist and pulled her to him, kissing her again.

Did You Enjoy This Book?

If you liked reading this book and have time, any review on www.amazon.co.uk or www.amazon.com would be appreciated and it would be good to meet up with any readers on my facebook page at www.facebook.com/richardclarkbooks.

Printed in Dunstable, United Kingdom

64841776R00133